DOUGLAS ADAMS

The Hitchhiker's Guide to the Galaxy

PUBLISHED BY POCKET BOOKS NEW YORK

**POCKET BOOKS, a Simon & Schuster division of
GULF & WESTERN CORPORATION**
1230 Avenue of the Americas, New York, N.Y. 10020

for Jonny Brock and Clare Gorst
and all other Arlingtonians
for tea, sympathy and a sofa

The Hitchhiker's Guide to the Galaxy

Far out in the uncharted backwaters of the unfashionable end of the Western Spiral arm of the Galaxy lies a small unregarded yellow sun.

Orbiting this at a distance of roughly ninety-eight million miles is an utterly insignificant little blue-green planet whose ape-descended life forms are so amazingly primitive that they still think digital watches are a pretty neat idea.

This planet has—or rather had—a problem, which was this: most of the people living on it were unhappy for pretty much of the time. Many solutions were suggested for this problem, but most of these were largely concerned with the movements of small green pieces of paper, which is odd because on the whole it wasn't the small green pieces of paper that were unhappy.

And so the problem remained; lots of the people were mean, and most of them were miserable, even the ones with digital watches.

Many were increasingly of the opinion that they'd all made a big mistake in coming down from the trees in the first place. And some said that even the trees had been a bad move, and that no one should ever have left the oceans.

And then, one Thursday, nearly two thousand years after one man had been nailed to a tree for saying how great it would be to be nice to people for a change, a girl sitting on her own in a small cafe in Rickmansworth suddenly realized what it was that had been going wrong all this time, and she finally knew how the world could be made a good and happy place. This time it was right, it would work, and no one would have to get nailed to anything.

Sadly, however, before she could get to a phone to tell anyone about it, a terrible, stupid catastrophe occurred, and the idea was lost for ever.

This is not her story.

But it is the story of that terrible, stupid catastrophe and some of its consequences.

It is also the story of a book, a book called The Hitchhiker's Guide to the Galaxy—not an Earth book, never published on Earth, and until the terrible catastrophe occurred, never seen or even heard of by any Earthman.

Nevertheless, a wholly remarkable book.

In fact, it was probably the most remarkable book ever to come out of the great publishing corporations of Ursa Minor—of which no Earthman had ever heard either.

Not only is it a wholly remarkable book, it is also a highly successful one—more popular than the Celestial Home Care Omnibus, better selling than Fifty-three More Things to Do in Zero Gravity, and more controversial than Oolon Colluphid's trilogy of philosophical blockbusters, Where God Went Wrong, Some More of God's Greatest Mistakes and Who Is This God Person Anyway?

In many of the more relaxed civilizations on the Outer Eastern Rim of the Galaxy, the Hitchhiker's Guide has already supplanted the great Encyclopedia Galactica as the standard repository of all knowledge and wisdom, for though it has many omissions and contains much that is apocryphal, or at least wildly inaccurate, it scores over the older, more pedestrian work in two important respects.

First, it is slightly cheaper; and second, it has the words DON'T PANIC inscribed in large friendly letters on its cover.

But the story of this terrible, stupid Thursday, the story of its extraordinary consequences, and the story of how these consequences are inextricably intertwined with this remarkable book begins very simply.

It begins with a house.

Chapter 1

The house stood on a slight rise just on the edge of the village. It stood on its own and looked out over a broad spread of West Country farmland. Not a remarkable house by any means—it was about thirty years old, squattish, squarish, made of brick, and had four windows set in the front of a size and proportion which more or less exactly failed to please the eye.

The only person for whom the house was in any way special was Arthur Dent, and that was only because it happened to be the one he lived in. He had lived in it for about three years, ever since he had moved out of London because it made him nervous and irritable. He was about thirty as well, tall, dark-haired and never quite at ease with himself. The thing that used to worry him most was the fact that people always used to ask him what he was looking so worried about. He worked in local radio which he always used to tell his friends was a lot more interesting than they probably thought. It was, too—most of his friends worked in advertising.

On Wednesday night it had rained very heavily, the lane was wet and muddy, but the Thursday morning sun was bright and clear as it shone on Arthur Dent's house for what was to be the last time.

It hadn't properly registered yet with Arthur that the council wanted to knock it down and build a bypass instead.

At eight o'clock on Thursday morning Arthur didn't feel very good. He woke up blearily, got up, wandered blearily round his room, opened a window, saw a bulldozer, found his slippers, and stomped off to the bathroom to wash.

Toothpaste on the brush—so. Scrub.

Shaving mirror—pointing at the ceiling. He adjusted it. For a moment it reflected a second bulldozer through the bathroom window. Properly adjusted, it reflected Arthur Dent's bristles. He shaved them off, washed, dried and stomped off to the kitchen to find something pleasant to put in his mouth.

Kettle, plug, fridge, milk, coffee. Yawn.

The word *bulldozer* wandered through his mind for a moment in search of something to connect with.

The bulldozer outside the kitchen window was quite a big one.

He stared at it.

"Yellow," he thought, and stomped off back to his bedroom to get dressed.

Passing the bathroom he stopped to drink a large glass of water, and another. He began to suspect that he was hung over. Why was he hung over? Had he been drinking the night before? He supposed that he must have been. He caught a glint in the shaving mirror. "Yellow," he thought, and stomped on to the bedroom.

He stood and thought. The pub, he thought. Oh dear, the pub. He vaguely remembered being angry, angry about something that seemed important. He'd been telling people about it, telling people about it at great length, he rather suspected: his clearest visual recollection was of glazed looks on other people's faces. Something about a new bypass he'd just found out about. It had been in the pipeline for months only no one seemed to have known about it. Ridiculous. He took a swig of water. It would sort itself out, he'd decided, no one wanted a bypass, the council didn't have a leg to stand on. It would sort itself out.

God, what a terrible hangover it had earned him though. He looked at himself in the wardrobe mirror. He stuck out his tongue. "Yellow," he thought. The word *yellow* wandered through his mind in search of something to connect with.

Fifteen seconds later he was out of the house and lying in front of a big yellow bulldozer that was advancing up his garden path.

Mr. L. Prosser was, as they say, only human. In other words he was a carbon-based bipedal life form descended from an ape. More specifically he was forty, fat and shabby and worked for the local council. Curiously enough, though he didn't know it, he was also a direct male-line descendant of Genghis Khan, though intervening generations and racial mixing had so juggled his genes that he had no discernible Mongoloid characteristics, and the only vestiges left in Mr. L. Prosser of his mighty ancestry were a pronounced stoutness about the tum and a predilection for little fur hats.

He was by no means a great warrior; in fact he was a nervous, worried man. Today he was particularly nervous and worried because something had gone seriously wrong with his job, which was to see that Arthur Dent's house got cleared out of the way before the day was out.

"Come off it, Mr. Dent," he said, "you can't win, you know. You can't lie in front of the bulldozer indefinitely." He tried to make his eyes blaze fiercely but they just wouldn't do it.

Arthur lay in the mud and squelched at him.

"I'm game," he said, "we'll see who rusts first."

"I'm afraid you're going to have to accept it," said Mr. Prosser, gripping his fur hat and rolling it round the top of his head; "this bypass has got to be built and it's going to be built!"

"First I've heard of it," said Arthur, "why's it got to be built?"

Mr. Prosser shook his finger at him for a bit, then stopped and put it away again.

"What do you mean, why's it got to be built?" he said. "It's a bypass. You've got to build bypasses."

Bypasses are devices that allow some people to dash from point A to point B very fast while other people dash from point B to point A very fast. People living at point C, being a point directly in between, are often given to wonder what's so great about point A that so many people from point B are so keen to get there, and what's so great about point B that so many people from point A are so keen to get there. They often wish that people would just once and for all work out where the hell they wanted to be.

Mr. Prosser wanted to be at point D. Point D wasn't anywhere in particular, it was just any convenient point a very long way from points A, B and C. He would have a nice little cottage at point D, with axes over the door, and spend a pleasant amount of time at point E, which would be the nearest pub to point D. His wife of course wanted climbing roses, but he wanted axes. He didn't know why—he just liked axes. He flushed hotly under the derisive grins of the bulldozer drivers.

He shifted his weight from foot to foot, but it was equally uncomfortable on each. Obviously somebody had been appallingly incompetent and he hoped to God it wasn't him.

Mr. Prosser said, "You were quite entitled to make any suggestions or protests at the appropriate time, you know."

"Appropriate time?" hooted Arthur. "Appropriate time? The first I knew about it was when a workman arrived at my home yesterday. I asked him if he'd come to clean the windows and he said no, he'd come to demolish the house. He didn't tell me straight away of course. Oh no. First he wiped a couple of windows and charged me a fiver. Then he told me."

"But Mr. Dent, the plans have been available in the local planning office for the last nine months."

"Oh yes, well, as soon as I heard I went straight round to see them, yesterday afternoon. You hadn't exactly gone out of your way to call attention to them, had you? I mean, like actually telling anybody or anything."

"But the plans were on display . . ."

"On display? I eventually had to go down to the cellar to find them."

"That's the display department."

"With a flashlight."

"Ah, well, the lights had probably gone."

"So had the stairs."

"But look, you found the notice, didn't you?"

"Yes," said Arthur, "yes I did. It was on display in the bottom of a locked filing cabinet stuck in a disused lavatory with a sign on the door saying 'Beware of the Leopard.' "

A cloud passed overhead. It cast a shadow over Arthur Dent as he lay propped up on his elbow in the cold mud. It cast a shadow over Arthur Dent's house. Mr. Prosser frowned at it.

"It's not as if it's a particularly nice house," he said.

"I'm sorry, but I happen to like it."

"You'll like the bypass."

"Oh, shut up," said Arthur Dent. "Shut up and go away, and take your bloody bypass with you. You haven't got a leg to stand on and you know it."

Mr. Prosser's mouth opened and closed a couple of times while his mind was for a moment filled with inexplicable but terribly attractive visions of Arthur Dent's house being consumed with fire and Arthur himself running screaming from the blazing ruin with at least three hefty spears protruding from his back. Mr. Prosser was often bothered with visions like these and they made him feel very nervous. He stuttered for a moment and then pulled himself together.

"Mr. Dent," he said.

"Hello? Yes?" said Arthur.

"Some factual information for you. Have you any idea how much damage that bulldozer would suffer if I just let it roll straight over you?"

"How much?" said Arthur.

"None at all," said Mr. Prosser, and stormed nervously off wondering why his brain was filled with a thousand hairy horsemen all shouting at him.

By a curious coincidence, "None at all" is exactly how much suspicion the ape-descendant Arthur Dent had that one of his closest friends was not descended from an ape, but was in fact from a small planet somewhere in the vicinity of Betelgeuse and not from Guildford as he usually claimed.

Arthur Dent had never, ever suspected this.

This friend of his had first arrived on the planet Earth some fifteen Earth years previously, and he had worked hard to blend himself into Earth society—with, it must be said, some success. For instance, he had spent those fifteen years pretending to be an out-of-work actor, which was plausible enough.

He had made one careless blunder though, because he had skimped a bit on his preparatory research. The information he had gathered had led him to choose the name "Ford Prefect" as being nicely inconspicuous.

He was not conspicuously tall, his features were striking but not conspicuously handsome. His hair was wiry and gingerish and brushed backward from the temples. His skin seemed to be pulled backward from the nose. There was something very slightly odd about him, but it was difficult to say what it was. Perhaps it was that his eyes didn't seem to blink often enough and when you talked to him for any length of time your eyes began involuntarily to water on his behalf. Perhaps it was that he smiled slightly too broadly and gave people the unnerving impression that he was about to go for their neck.

He struck most of the friends he had made on Earth as an eccentric, but a harmless one—an unruly boozer with some oddish habits. For instance, he would often gate-crash university parties, get badly drunk and start making fun of any astrophysicists he could find till he got thrown out.

Sometimes he would get seized with oddly distracted moods and stare into the sky as if hypnotized until someone asked him what he was doing. Then he would start guiltily for a moment, relax and grin.

"Oh, just looking for flying saucers," he would joke, and everyone would laugh and ask him what sort of flying saucers he was looking for.

"Green ones!" he would reply with a wicked grin, laugh wildly for a moment and then suddenly lunge for the nearest bar and buy an enormous round of drinks.

Evenings like this usually ended badly. Ford would get out of his skull on whisky, huddle in a corner with some girl and explain to her in slurred phrases that honestly the color of the flying saucers didn't matter that much really.

Thereafter, staggering semiparalytic down the night streets, he would often ask passing policemen if they knew the way to Betelgeuse. The policemen would usually say something like, "Don't you think it's about time you went off home, sir?"

"I'm trying to, baby, I'm trying to," is what Ford invariably replied on these occasions.

In fact what he was really looking for when he stared distractedly into the sky was any kind of flying saucer at all.

The reason he said green was that green was the traditional space livery of the Betelgeuse trading scouts.

Ford Prefect was desperate that any flying saucer at all would arrive soon because fifteen years was a long time to get stranded anywhere, particularly somewhere as mind-bogglingly dull as the Earth.

Ford wished that a flying saucer would arrive soon because he knew how to flag flying saucers down and get lifts from them. He knew how to see the Marvels of the Universe for less than thirty Altairian dollars a day.

In fact, Ford Prefect was a roving researcher for that wholly remarkable book, *The Hitchhiker's Guide to the Galaxy*.

Human beings are great adapters, and by lunchtime life in the environs of Arthur's house had settled into a steady routine. It was Arthur's accepted role to lie squelching in the mud making occasional demands to see his lawyer, his mother or a good book; it was Mr. Prosser's accepted role to tackle Arthur with the occasional new ploy such as the For the Public Good talk, or the March of Progress talk, the They Knocked My House Down Once You Know, Never Looked Back talk and various other cajoleries and threats; and it was the bulldozer drivers' accepted role to sit around drinking coffee and experimenting with union regulations to see how they could turn the situation to their financial advantage.

The Earth moved slowly in its diurnal course.

The sun was beginning to dry out the mud that Arthur lay in.

A shadow moved across him again.

"Hello, Arthur," said the shadow.

Arthur looked up and squinting into the sun was startled to see Ford Prefect standing above him.

"Ford! Hello, how are you?"

"Fine," said Ford, "look, are you busy?"

"Am I *busy?*" exclaimed Arthur. "Well, I've just got all these bulldozers and things to lie in front of because they'll knock my house down if I don't, but other than that . . . well, no, not especially, why?"

They don't have sarcasm on Betelgeuse, and Ford Prefect often failed to notice it unless he was concentrating. He said, "Good, is there anywhere we can talk?"

"What?" said Arthur Dent.

For a few seconds Ford seemed to ignore him, and stared fixedly into the sky like a rabbit trying to get run over by a car. Then suddenly he squatted down beside Arthur.

"We've got to talk," he said urgently.

"Fine," said Arthur, "talk."

"And drink," said Ford. "It's vitally important that we talk and drink. Now. We'll go to the pub in the village."

He looked into the sky again, nervous, expectant.

"Look, don't you understand?" shouted Arthur. He pointed at Prosser. "That man wants to knock my house down!"

Ford glanced at him, puzzled.

"Well, he can do it while you're away, can't he?" he asked.

"But I don't want him to!"

"Ah."

"Look, what's the matter with you, Ford?" said Arthur.

"Nothing. Nothing's the matter. Listen to me—I've got to tell you the most important thing you've ever heard. I've got to tell you now, and I've got to tell you in the saloon bar of the Horse and Groom."

"But why?"

"Because you're going to need a very stiff drink."

Ford stared at Arthur, and Arthur was astonished to find his will beginning to weaken. He didn't realize that this was because of an old drinking game that Ford learned to play in the hyperspace ports that served the madranite mining belts in the star system of Orion Beta.

The game was not unlike the Earth game called Indian wrestling, and was played like this:

Two contestants would sit either side of a table, with a glass in front of each of them.

Between them would be placed a bottle of Janx Spirit (as immortalized in that ancient Orion mining song, "Oh, don't give me none more of that Old Janx Spirit/No, don't you give me none more of that Old Janx Spirit/For my head will fly, my tongue will lie, my eyes will fry and I may die/Won't you pour me one more of that sinful Old Janx Spirit").

Each of the two contestants would then concentrate their will on the bottle and attempt to tip it and pour spirit into the glass of his opponent, who would then have to drink it.

The bottle would then be refilled. The game would be played again. And again.

Once you started to lose you would probably keep losing, because one of the effects of Janx Spirit is to depress tele-psychic power.

As soon as a predetermined quantity had been consumed, the final loser would have to perform a forfeit, which was usually obscenely biological.

Ford Prefect usually played to lose.

Ford stared at Arthur, who began to think that perhaps he did want to go to the Horse and Groom after all.

"But what about my house . . .?" he asked plaintively.

Ford looked across to Mr. Prosser, and suddenly a wicked thought struck him.

"He wants to knock your house down?"

"Yes, he wants to build . . ."

"And he can't because you're lying in front of his bulldozer?"

"Yes, and . . ."

"I'm sure we can come to some arrangement," said Ford. "Excuse me!" he shouted.

Mr. Prosser (who was arguing with a spokesman for the bulldozer drivers about whether or not Arthur Dent constituted a mental health hazard, and how much they should get paid if he did) looked around. He was surprised and slightly alarmed to see that Arthur had company.

"Yes? Hello?" he called. "Has Mr. Dent come to his senses yet?"

"Can we for the moment," called Ford, "assume that he hasn't?"

"Well?" sighed Mr. Prosser.

"And can we also assume," said Ford, "that he's going to be staying here all day?"

"So?"

"So all your men are going to be standing around all day doing nothing?"

"Could be, could be . . ."

"Well, if you're resigned to doing that anyway, you don't actually need him to lie here all the time do you?"

"What?"

"You don't," said Ford patiently, "actually need him here."

Mr. Prosser thought about this.

"Well, no, not as such . . ." he said, "not exactly *need* . . ."

Prosser was worried. He thought that one of them wasn't making a lot of sense.

Ford said, "So if you would just like to take it as read that he's actually here, then he and I could slip off down to the pub for half an hour. How does that sound?"

Mr. Prosser thought it sounded perfectly potty.

"That sounds perfectly reasonable . . ." he said in a reassuring tone of voice, wondering who he was trying to reassure.

"And if you want to pop off for a quick one yourself later on," said Ford, "we can always cover for you in return."

"Thank you very much," said Mr. Prosser, who no longer knew how to play this at all, "thank you very much, yes, that's very kind . . ." He frowned, then smiled, then tried to do both at once, failed, grasped hold of his fur hat and rolled it fitfully round the top of his head. He could only assume that he had just won.

"So," continued Ford Prefect, "if you would just like to come over here and lie down . . ."

"What?" said Mr. Prosser.

"Ah, I'm sorry," said Ford, "perhaps I hadn't made myself fully clear. Somebody's got to lie in front of the bulldozers, haven't they? Or there won't be anything to stop them driving into Mr. Dent's house, will there?"

"What?" said Mr. Prosser again.

"It's very simple," said Ford, "my client, Mr. Dent, says that he will stop lying here in the mud on the sole condition that you come and take over from him."

"What are you talking about?" said Arthur, but Ford nudged him with his shoe to be quiet.

"You want me," said Prosser, spelling out this new thought to himself, "to come and lie there . . ."

"Yes."

"In front of the bulldozer?"

"Yes."

"Instead of Mr. Dent."

"Yes."

"In the mud."

"In, as you say, the mud."

As soon as Mr. Prosser realized that he was substantially the loser after all, it was as if a weight lifted itself off his shoulders: this was more like the world as he knew it. He sighed.

"In return for which you will take Mr. Dent with you down to the pub?"

"That's it," said Ford, "that's it exactly."

Mr. Prosser took a few nervous steps forward and stopped.

"Promise?" he said.

"Promise," said Ford. He turned to Arthur.

"Come on," he said to him, "get up and let the man lie down."

Arthur stood up, feeling as if he was in a dream.

Ford beckoned to Prosser, who sadly, awkwardly, sat down in the mud. He felt that his whole life was some kind of dream and he sometimes wondered whose it was and whether they were enjoying it. The mud folded itself round his bottom and his arms and oozed into his shoes.

Ford looked at him severely.

"And no sneaky knocking Mr. Dent's house down while he's away, all right? he said.

"The mere thought," growled Mr. Prosser, "hadn't even begun to speculate," he continued, settling himself back, "about the merest possibility of crossing my mind."

He saw the bulldozer drivers' union representative approaching and let his head sink back and closed his eyes. He was trying to marshal his arguments for proving that he did not now constitute a mental health hazard himself. He was far from certain about this—his mind seemed to be full of noise, horses, smoke and the stench of blood. This always happened when he felt miserable or put upon, and he had never been able to explain it to himself. In a high dimension of which we know nothing, the mighty Khan bellowed with rage, but Mr. Prosser only trembled slightly and whimpered. He began to feel little pricks of water behind his eyelids. Bureaucratic cock-ups, angry men lying in mud, indecipherable strangers handing out inexplicable humiliation and an unidentified army of horsemen laughing at him in his head—what a day.

What a day. Ford Prefect knew that it didn't matter a pair of dingo's kidneys whether Arthur's house got knocked down or not now.

Arthur remained very worried.

"But can we trust him?" he said.

"Myself I'd trust him to the end of the Earth," said Ford.

"Oh yes," said Arthur, "and how far's that?"

"About twelve minutes away," said Ford, "come on, I need a drink."

Chapter 2

Here's what the Encyclopedia Galactica *has to say about alcohol. It says that alcohol is a colorless volatile liquid formed by the fermentation of sugars and also notes its intoxicating effect on certain carbon-based life forms.*

The Hitchhiker's Guide to the Galaxy *also mentions alcohol. It says that the best drink in existence is the Pan Galactic Gargle Blaster.*

It says that the effect of drinking a Pan Galactic Gargle Blaster is like having your brains smashed out by a slice of lemon wrapped round a large gold brick.

The *Guide also tells you on which planets the best Pan Galactic Gargle Blasters are mixed, how much you can expect to pay for one and what voluntary organizations exist to help you rehabilitate afterward.*

The *Guide even tells you how you can mix one yourself.*

Take the juice from one bottle of the Ol' Janx Spirit, it says.

Pour into it one measure of water from the seas of Santraginus V—Oh, that Santraginean seawater, it says. Oh, those Santraginean fish!

Allow three cubes of Arcturan Mega-gin to melt into the mixture (it must be properly iced or the benzine is lost).

Allow four liters of Fallian marsh gas to bubble through it, in memory of all those happy hikers who have died of pleasure in the Marshes of Fallia.

Over the back of a silver spoon float a measure of Qualactin Hypermint extract, redolent of all the heady odors of the dark Qualactin Zones, subtle, sweet and mystic.

Drop in the tooth of an Algolian Suntiger. Watch it dissolve, spreading the fires of the Algolian Suns deep into the heart of the drink.

Sprinkle Zamphuor.

Add an olive.

Drink . . . but . . . very carefully . . .

The Hitchhiker's Guide to the Galaxy *sells rather better than the* Encyclopedia Galactica.

"Six pints of bitter," said Ford Prefect to the barman of the Horse and Groom. "And quickly please, the world's about to end."

The barman of the Horse and Groom didn't deserve this sort of treatment; he was a dignified old man. He pushed his glasses up his nose and blinked at Ford Prefect. Ford ignored him and stared out the window, so the barman looked instead at Arthur, who shrugged helplessly and said nothing.

So the barman said, "Oh yes, sir? Nice weather for it," and started pulling pints.

He tried again. "Going to watch the match this afternoon then?"

Ford glanced round at him.

"No, no point," he said, and looked back out the window.

"What's that, foregone conclusion then, you reckon, sir?" said the barman. "Arsenal without a chance?"

"No no," said Ford, "it's just that the world's about to end."

"Oh yes, sir, so you said," said the barman, looking over his glasses this time at Arthur. "Lucky escape for Arsenal if it did."

Ford looked back at him, genuinely surprised.

"No, not really," he said. He frowned.

The barman breathed in heavily. "There you are, sir, six pints," he said.

Arthur smiled at him wanly and shrugged again. He turned and smiled wanly at the rest of the pub just in case any of them had heard what was going on.

None of them had, and none of them could understand what he was smiling at them for.

A man sitting next to Ford at the bar looked at the two men, looked at the six pints, did a swift burst of mental arithmetic, arrived at an answer he liked and grinned a stupid hopeful grin at them.

"Get off," said Ford, "they're ours," giving him a look that would have made an Algolian Suntiger get on with what it was doing.

Ford slapped a five-pound note on the bar. He said, "Keep the change."

"What, from a fiver? Thank you, sir."

"You've got ten minutes left to spend it."

The barman decided simply to walk away for a bit.

"Ford," said Arthur, "would you please tell me what the hell is going on?"

"Drink up," said Ford, "you've got three pints to get through."

"Three pints?" said Arthur. "At lunchtime?"

The man next to Ford grinned and nodded happily. Ford ignored him. He said, "Time is an illusion. Lunchtime doubly so."

"Very deep," said Arthur, "you should send that in to the *Reader's Digest*. They've got a page for people like you."

"Drink up."

"Why three pints all of a sudden?"

"Muscle relaxant, you'll need it."

"Muscle relaxant?"

"Muscle relaxant."

Arthur stared into his beer.

"Did I do anything wrong today," he said, "or has the world always been like this and I've been too wrapped up in myself to notice?"

"All right," said Ford, "I'll try to explain. How long have we known each other?"

"How long?" Arthur thought. "Er, about five years, maybe six," he said. "Most of it seemed to make some kind of sense at the time."

"All right," said Ford. "How would you react if I said that I'm not from Guildford after all, but from a small planet somewhere in the vicinity of Betelgeuse?"

Arthur shrugged in a so-so sort of way.

"I don't know," he said, taking a pull of beer. "Why, do you think it's the sort of thing you're likely to say?"

Ford gave up. It really wasn't worth bothering at the

moment, what with the world being about to end. He just said, "Drink up."

He added, perfectly factually, "The world's about to end."

Arthur gave the rest of the pub another wan smile. The rest of the pub frowned at him. A man waved at him to stop smiling at them and mind his own business.

"This must be Thursday," said Arthur to himself, sinking low over his beer. "I never could get the hang of Thursdays."

Chapter 3

On this particular Thursday, something was moving quietly through the ionosphere many miles above the surface of the planet; several somethings in fact, several dozen huge yellow chunky slablike somethings, huge as office blocks, silent as birds. They soared with ease, basking in electromagnetic rays from the star Sol, biding their time, grouping, preparing.

The planet beneath them was almost perfectly oblivious of their presence, which was just how they wanted it for the moment. The huge yellow something went unnoticed at Goonhilly, they passed over Cape Canaveral without a blip, Woomera and Jodrell Bank looked straight through them, which was a pity because it was exactly the sort of thing they'd been looking for all these years.

The only place they registered at all was on a small black device called a Sub-Etha Sens-O-Matic which winked away quietly to itself. It nestled in the darkness inside a leather satchel which Ford Prefect habitually wore slung around his neck. The contents of Ford Prefect's satchel were quite interesting in fact and would have made any Earth physicist's eyes pop out of his head, which is why he always concealed them by keeping a couple of dogeared scripts for plays he pretended he was auditioning for stuffed in the top. Besides the Sub-Etha Sens-O-Matic and the scripts he had an Electronic Thumb—a short squat black rod, smooth and matt with a couple of flat switches and dials at one end; he also had a device that looked rather like a largish electronic calculator. This had about a hundred tiny flat press buttons and a screen about four inches square on which any one of a million "pages" could be summoned at a moment's notice. It looked insanely complicated, and this was one of the reasons why the snug plastic cover it fitted into had the words DON'T PANIC printed on it in large friendly letters. The other reason was that this device was in fact that most remarkable of all books ever to come out of the great publishing corporations of Ursa Minor—*The Hitchhiker's Guide to the Galaxy*. The reason why it was published in the form of a micro sub meson electronic component is that if it were printed in normal book form, an interstellar hitchhiker would require several inconveniently large buildings to carry it around in.

Beneath that in Ford Prefect's satchel were a few ballpoints, a notepad and a largish bath towel from Marks and Spencer.

The Hitchhiker's Guide to the Galaxy *has a few things to say on the subject of towels.*

A towel, it says, is about the most massively useful thing an interstellar hitchhiker can have. Partly it has great practical value. You can wrap it around you for warmth as you bound across the cold moons of Jaglan Beta; you can lie on it on the brilliant marble-sanded beaches of Santraginus V, inhaling the heady sea vapors; you can sleep under it beneath the stars which shine so redly on the desert world of Kakrafoon; use it to sail a miniraft down the slow heavy River Moth; wet it for use in hand-to-hand combat; wrap it round your head to ward off noxious fumes or avoid the gaze of the Ravenous Bugblatter Beast of Traal (a mind-bogglingly stupid animal, it assumes that if you can't see it, it can't see you—daft as a brush, but very very ravenous); you can wave your towel in emergencies as a distress signal, and of course dry yourself off with it if it still seems to be clean enough.

More importantly, a towel has immense psychological value. For some reason, if a strag (strag: nonhitchhiker) discovers that a hitchhiker has his towel with him, he will automatically assume that he is also in possession of a toothbrush, washcloth, soap, tin of biscuits, flask, compass, map, ball of string, gnat spray, wet-weather gear, space suit etc., etc. Furthermore, the strag will then happily lend the hitchhiker any of these or a dozen other items that the hitchhiker might accidentally have "lost." What the strag will think is that any man who can hitch the length and breadth of the Galaxy, rough it, slum it, struggle against terrible odds, win through and still know where his towel is, is clearly a man to be reckoned with.

Hence a phrase that has passed into hitchhiking slang, as in "Hey, you sass that hoopy Ford Prefect? There's a frood who really knows where his towel is." (Sass: know, be aware of, meet, have sex with; hoopy: really together guy; frood: really amazingly together guy.)

Nestling quietly on top of the towel in Ford Prefect's satchel, the Sub-Etha Sens-O-Matic began to wink more quickly. Miles above the surface of the planet the huge yellow somethings began to fan out. At Jodrell Bank, someone decided it was time for a nice relaxing cup of tea.

"You got a towel with you?" said Ford suddenly to Arthur.

Arthur, struggling through his third pint, looked round at him.

"Why? What, no . . . should I have?" He had given up being surprised, there didn't seem to be any point any longer.

Ford clicked his tongue in irritation.

"Drink up," he urged.

At that moment the dull sound of a rumbling crash from outside filtered through the low murmur of the pub, through the sound of the jukebox, through the sound of the man next to Ford hiccupping over the whisky Ford had eventually bought him.

Arthur choked on his beer, leaped to his feet.

"What's that?" he yelped.

"Don't worry," said Ford, "they haven't started yet."

"Thank God for that," said Arthur, and relaxed.

"It's probably just your house being knocked down," said Ford, downing his last pint.

"What?" shouted Arthur. Suddenly Ford's spell was broken. Arthur looked wildly around him and ran to the window.

"My God, they are! They're knocking my house down. What the hell am I doing in the pub, Ford?"

"It hardly makes any difference at this stage," said Ford, "let them have their fun."

"Fun?" yelped Arthur. "Fun!" He quickly checked out the window again that they were talking about the same thing.

"Damn their fun!" he hooted, and ran out of the pub furiously waving a nearly empty beer glass. He made no friends at all in the pub that lunchtime.

"Stop, you vandals! You home wreckers!" bawled Arthur. "You half-crazed Visigoths, stop, will you!"

Ford would have to go after him. Turning quickly to the barman he asked for four packets of peanuts.

"There you are, sir," said the barman, slapping the packets on the bar, "twenty-eight pence if you'd be so kind."

Ford was very kind—he gave the barman another five-pound note and told him to keep the change. The barman looked at it and then looked at Ford. He suddenly shivered: he experienced a momentary sensation that he didn't understand because no one on Earth had ever experienced it before. In moments of great stress, every life form that exists gives out a tiny subliminal signal. This signal simply communicates an exact and almost pathetic sense of how far that being is from the place of his birth. On Earth it is never possible to be farther than sixteen thousand miles from your birthplace, which really isn't very far, so such signals are too minute to be noticed. Ford Prefect was at this moment under great stress, and he was born six hundred light-years away in the near vicinity of Betelgeuse.

The barman reeled for a moment, hit by a shocking, incomprehensible sense of distance. He didn't know what it meant, but he looked at Ford Prefect with a new sense of respect, almost awe.

"Are you serious, sir?" he said in a small whisper which had the effect of silencing the pub. "You think the world's going to end?"

"Yes," said Ford.

"But, this afternoon."

Ford had recovered himself. He was at his flippest.

"Yes," he said gaily, "in less than two minutes I would estimate."

The barman couldn't believe this conversation he was having, but he couldn't believe the sensation he had just had either.

"Isn't there anything we can do about it then?" he said.

"No, nothing," said Ford, stuffing the peanuts into his pocket.

Someone in the hushed bar suddenly laughed raucously at how stupid everyone had become.

The man sitting next to Ford was a bit sozzled by now. His eyes weaved their way up to Ford.

"I thought," he said "that if the world was going to end we were meant to lie down or put a paper bag over our head or something."

"If you like, yes," said Ford.

"That's what they told us in the army," said the man, and his eyes began the long trek back toward his whisky.

"Will that help?" asked the barman.

"No," said Ford, and gave him a friendly smile. "Excuse me," he said, "I've got to go." With a wave, he left.

The pub was silent for a moment longer and then, embarrassingly enough, the man with the raucous laugh did it again. The girl he had dragged along to the pub with him had grown to loathe him dearly over the last hour, and it would probably have been a great satisfaction to her to know that in a minute and a half or so he would suddenly evaporate into a whiff of hydrogen, ozone and carbon monoxide. However, when the moment came she would be too busy evaporating herself to notice it.

The barman cleared his throat. He heard himself say, "Last orders, please."

The huge yellow machines began to sink downward and to move faster.

Ford knew they were there. This wasn't the way he had wanted it.

Running up the lane, Arthur had nearly reached his house. He didn't notice how cold it had suddenly become, he didn't notice the wind, he didn't notice the sudden irrational squall of rain. He didn't notice anything but the caterpillar bulldozers crawling over the rubble that had been his home.

"You barbarians!" he yelled. "I'll sue the council for every penny it's got! I'll have you hung, drawn and quartered! And whipped! And boiled . . . until . . . until . . . until you've had enough."

Ford was running after him very fast. Very very fast.

"And then I will do it again!" yelled Arthur. "And when I've finished I will take all the little bits, and I will *jump* on them!"

Arthur didn't notice that the men were running from the bulldozers; he didn't notice that Mr. Prosser was staring hectically into the sky. What Mr. Prosser had noticed was that huge yellow somethings were screaming through the clouds. Impossibly huge yellow somethings.

"And I will carry on jumping on them," yelled Arthur, still running, "until I get blisters, or I can think of anything even more unpleasant to do, and then . . ."

Arthur tripped, and fell headlong, rolled and landed flat on his back. At last he noticed that something was going on. His finger shot upward.

"What the hell's that?" he shrieked.

Whatever it was raced across the sky in its monstrous yellowness, tore the sky apart with mind-boggling noise and leaped off into the distance leaving the gaping air to shut behind it with a *bang* that drove your ears six feet into your skull.

Another one followed and did exactly the same thing only louder.

It's difficult to say exactly what the people on the surface of the planet were doing now, because they didn't really know what they were doing themselves. None of it made a lot of sense—running into houses, running out of houses, howling noiselessly at the noise. All around the world city streets exploded with people, cars skidded into each other as the noise fell on them and then rolled off like a tidal wave over hills and valleys, deserts and oceans, seeming to flatten everything it hit.

Only one man stood and watched the sky, stood with terrible sadness in his eyes and rubber bungs in his ears. He knew exactly what was happening and had known ever since his Sub-Etha Sens-O-Matic had started winking in the dead of night beside his pillow and wakened him with a start. It was what he had waited for all these years, but when he had deciphered the signal pattern sitting alone in his small dark room, a coldness had gripped him and squeezed his heart. Of all the races in all of the Galaxy who could have come and said a big hello to planet Earth, he thought, didn't it just have to be the Vogons.

Still, he knew what he had to do. As the Vogon craft screamed through the air high above him he opened his satchel. He threw away a copy of *Joseph and the Amazing Technicolor Dreamcoat*, he threw away a copy of *Godspell*: he wouldn't need them where he was going. Everything was ready, everything was prepared.

He knew where his towel was.

A sudden silence hit the Earth. If anything it was worse than the noise. For a while nothing happened.

The great ships hung motionless in the sky, over every nation on Earth. Motionless they hung, huge, heavy, steady in the sky, a blasphemy against nature. Many people went straight into shock as their minds tried to encompass what they were looking at. The ships hung in the sky in much the same way that bricks don't.

And still nothing happened.

Then there was a slight whisper, a sudden spacious whisper of open ambient sound. Every hi-fi set in the world, every radio, every television, every cassette recorder, every woofer, every tweeter, every mid-range driver in the world quietly turned itself on.

Every tin can, every dustbin, every window, every car, every wineglass, every sheet of rusty metal became activated as an acoustically perfect sounding board.

Before the Earth passed away it was going to be treated to the very ultimate in sound reproduction, the greatest public address system ever built. But there was no concert, no music, no fanfare, just a simple message.

"People of Earth, your attention, please," a voice said, and it was wonderful. Wonderful perfect quadrophonic sound with distortion levels so low as to make a brave man weep.

"This is Prostetnic Vogon Jeltz of the Galactic Hyperspace Planning Council," the voice continued. *"As you will no doubt be aware, the plans for development of the outlying regions of the Galaxy require the building of a hyperspatial express route through your star system, and regrettably your planet is one of those scheduled for demolition. The process will take slightly less than two of your Earth minutes. Thank you."*

The PA died away.

Uncomprehending terror settled on the watching people of Earth. The terror moved slowly through the gathered crowds as if they were iron filings on a sheet of board and a magnet was moving beneath them. Panic sprouted again, desperate fleeing panic, but there was nowhere to flee to.

Observing this, the Vogons turned on their PA again. It said:

"There's no point in acting all surprised about it. All the planning charts and demolition orders have been on display in your local planning department in Alpha Centauri for fifty of

your Earth years, so you've had plenty of time to lodge any formal complaint and it's far too late to start making a fuss about it now."

The PA fell silent again and its echo drifted off across the land. The huge ships turned slowly in the sky with easy power. On the underside of each a hatchway opened, an empty black square.

By this time somebody somewhere must have manned a radio transmitter, located a wavelength and broadcast a message back to the Vogon ships, to plead on behalf of the planet. Nobody ever heard what they said, they only heard the reply. The PA slammed back into life again. The voice was annoyed. It said:

"What do you mean, you've never been to Alpha Centauri? For heaven's sake, mankind, it's only four light-years away, you know. I'm sorry, but if you can't be bothered to take an interest in local affairs that's your own lookout.

"Energize the demolition beams."

Light poured out of the hatchways.

"I don't know," said the voice on the PA, *"apathetic bloody planet, I've no sympathy at all."* It cut off.

There was a terrible ghastly silence.

There was a terrible ghastly noise.

There was a terrible ghastly silence.

The Vogon Constructor Fleet coasted away into the inky starry void.

Chapter 4

ar away on the opposite spiral arm of the Galaxy, five hundred thousand light-years from the star Sol, Zaphod Beeblebrox, President of the Imperial Galactic Government, sped across the seas of Damogran, his ion drive delta boat winking and flashing in the Damogran sun.

Damogran the hot; Damogran the remote; Damogran the almost totally unheard of.

Damogran, secret home of the Heart of Gold.

The boat sped on across the water. It would be some time before it reached its destination because Damogran is such an inconveniently arranged planet. It consists of nothing but middling to large desert islands separated by very pretty but annoyingly wide stretches of ocean.

The boat sped on.

Because of this topographical awkwardness Damogran has always remained a deserted planet. This is why the Imperial Galactic Government chose Damogran for the Heart of Gold project, because it was so deserted and the Heart of Gold project was so secret.

The boat zipped and skipped across the sea, the sea that lay between the main islands of the only archipelago of any useful size on the whole planet. Zaphod Beeblebrox was on his way from the tiny spaceport on Easter Island (the name was an entirely meaningless coincidence—in Galacticspeke, *easter* means small, flat and light-brown) to the Heart of Gold island, which by another meaningless coincidence was called France.

One of the side effects of work on the Heart of Gold was a whole string of pretty meaningless coincidences.

But it was not in any way a coincidence that today, the day of culmination of the project, the great day of unveiling, the day that the Heart of Gold was finally to be introduced to a marveling Galaxy, was also a great day of culmination for Zaphod Beeblebrox. It was for the sake of this day that he had first decided to run for the presidency, a decision that had sent shock waves of astonishment throughout the Imperial Galaxy. Zaphod Beeblebrox? *President?* Not *the* Zaphod Beeblebrox? Not *the* President? Many had seen it as clinching proof that the whole of known creation had finally gone bananas.

Zaphod grinned and gave the boat an extra kick of speed.

Zaphod Beeblebrox, adventurer, ex-hippie, good-timer, (crook? quite possibly), manic self-publicist, terribly bad at personal relationships, often thought to be completely out to lunch.

President?

No one had gone bananas, not in that way at least.

Only six people in the entire Galaxy understood the principle on which the Galaxy was governed, and they knew that once Zaphod Beeblebrox had announced his intention to run as President it was more or less a fait accompli: he was ideal presidency fodder.*

What they completely failed to understand was why Zaphod was doing it.

He banked sharply, shooting a wild wall of water at the sun.

Today was the day; today was the day when they would realize what Zaphod had been up to. Today was what Zaphod Beeblebrox's presidency was all about. Today was also his two-hundredth birthday, but that was just another meaningless coincidence.

As he skipped his boat across the seas of Damogran he smiled quietly to himself about what a wonderful, exciting day it was going to be. He relaxed and spread his two arms lazily along the seat back. He steered with an extra arm

* President: full title President of the Imperial Galactic Government.

The term *Imperial* is kept though it is now an anachronism. The hereditary Emperor is nearly dead and has been for many centuries. In the last moments of his dying coma he was locked in a stasis field which keeps him in a state of perpetual unchangingness. All his heirs are now long dead, and this means that without any drastic political upheaval, power has simply and effectively moved a rung or two down the ladder, and is now seen to be vested in a body that used to act simply as advisers to the Emperor—an elected governmental assembly headed by a President elected by that assembly. In fact it vests in no such place.

The President in particular is very much a figurehead—he wields no real power whatsoever. He is apparently chosen by the government, but the qualities he is required to display are not those of leadership but those of finely judged outrage. For this reason the President is always a controversial choice, always an infuriating but fascinating character. His job is not to wield power but to draw attention away from it. On those criteria Zaphod Beeblebrox is one of the most successful Presidents the Galaxy has ever had—he has already spent two of his ten presidential years in prison for fraud. Very very few people realize that the President and the Government have virtually no power at all, and of these few people only six know whence ultimate political power is wielded. Most of the others secretly believe that the ultimate decision-making process is handled by a computer. They couldn't be more wrong.

he'd recently had fitted just beneath his right one to help improve his ski-boxing.

"Hey," he cooed to himself, "you're a real cool boy, you." But his nerves sang a song shriller than a dog whistle.

The island of France was about twenty miles long, five miles across the middle, sandy and crescent-shaped. In fact, it seemed to exist not so much as an island in its own right as simply a means of defining the sweep and curve of a huge bay. This impression was heightened by the fact that the inner coastline of the crescent consisted almost entirely of steep cliffs. From the top of the cliff the land sloped slowly down five miles to the opposite shore.

On top of the cliffs stood a reception committee.

It consisted in large part of the engineers and researchers who had built the Heart of Gold—mostly humanoid, but here and there were a few reptiloid atomineers, two or three green sylphlike maximegalaticians, an octopodic physucturalist or two and a Hooloovoo (a Hooloovoo is a superintelligent shade of the color blue). All except the Hooloovoo were resplendent in their multicolored ceremonial lab coats; the Hooloovoo had been temporarily refracted into a free-standing prism for the occasion.

There was a mood of immense excitement thrilling through all of them. Together and between them they had gone to and beyond the furthest limits of physical laws, restructured the fundamental fabric of matter, strained, twisted and broken the laws of possibility and impossibility, but still the greatest excitement of all seemed to be to meet a man with an orange sash round his neck. (An orange sash was what the President of the Galaxy traditionally wore.) It might not even have made much difference to them if they'd known exactly how much power the President of the Galaxy actually wielded: none at all. Only six people in the Galaxy knew that the job of the Galactic President was not to wield power but to attract attention away from it.

Zaphod Beeblebrox was amazingly good at his job.

The crowd gasped, dazzled by sun and seamanship, as the presidential speedboat zipped round the headland into the bay. It flashed and shone as it came skating over the sea in wide skidding turns.

In fact, it didn't need to touch the water at all, because it was supported on a hazy cushion of ionized atoms, but just for effect it was fitted with thin finblades which could be lowered into the water. They slashed sheets of water hissing into the air, carved deep gashes in the sea which swayed crazily and sank back foaming in the boat's wake as it careered across the bay.

Zaphod loved effect: it was what he was best at.

He twisted the wheel sharply, the boat skidded round in a wild scything skid beneath the cliff face and dropped to rest lightly on the rocking waves.

Within seconds he ran out onto the deck and waved and grinned at over three billion people. The three billion people weren't actually there, but they watched his every gesture through the eyes of a small robot tri-D camera which hovered obsequiously in the air nearby. The antics of the President always made amazingly popular tri-D: that's what they were for.

He grinned again. Three billion and six people didn't know it, but today would be a bigger antic than anyone had bargained for.

The robot camera homed in for a close-up on the more popular of his two heads and he waved again. He was roughly humanoid in appearance except for the extra head and third arm. His fair tousled hair stuck out in random directions, his blue eyes glinted with something completely unidentifiable, and his chins were almost always unshaven.

A twenty-foot-high transparent globe floated next to his boat, rolling and bobbing, glistening in the brilliant sun. Inside it floated a wide semicircular sofa upholstered in glorious red leather: the more the globe bobbed and rolled, the more the sofa stayed perfectly still, steady as an upholstered rock. Again, all done for effect as much as anything.

Zaphod stepped through the wall of the globe and relaxed on the sofa. He spread his two arms along the back and with the third brushed some dust off his knee. His heads looked about, smiling; he put his feet up. At any moment, he thought, he might scream.

Water boiled up beneath the bubble, it seethed and spouted. The bubble surged into the air, bobbing and rolling on the water spout. Up, up it climbed, throwing stilts of light at the cliff. Up it surged on the jet, the water falling from beneath it, crashing back into the sea hundreds of feet below.

Zaphod smiled, picturing himself.

A thoroughly ridiculous form of transport, but a thoroughly beautiful one.

At the top of the cliff the globe wavered for a moment,

tipped onto a railed ramp, rolled down it to a small concave platform and riddled to a halt.

To tremendous applause Zaphod Beeblebrox stepped out of the bubble, his orange sash blazing in the light.

The President of the Galaxy had arrived.

He waited for the applause to die down, then raised his hand in greeting.

"Hi," he said.

A government spider sidled up to him and attempted to press a copy of his prepared speech into his hands. Pages three to seven of the original version were at the moment floating soggily on the Damogran Sea some five miles out from the bay. Pages one and two had been salvaged by a Damogran Frond Crested Eagle and had already become incorporated into an extraordinary new form of nest which the eagle had invented. It was constructed largely of papier-mâché and it was virtually impossible for a newly hatched baby eagle to break out of it. The Damogran Frond Crested Eagle had heard of the notion of survival of the species but wanted no truck with it.

Zaphod Beeblebrox would not be needing his set speech and he gently deflected the one being offered him by the spider.

"Hi," he said again.

Everyone beamed at him, or at least, nearly everyone. He singled out Trillian from the crowd. Trillian was a girl that Zaphod had picked up recently while visiting a planet, just for fun, incognito. She was slim, darkish, humanoid, with long waves of black hair, a full mouth, an odd little knob of a nose and ridiculously brown eyes. With her red head scarf knotted in that particular way and her long flowing silky brown dress, she looked vaguely Arabic. Not that anyone there had ever heard of an Arab of course. The Arabs had very recently ceased to exist, and even when they had existed they were five hundred thousand light-years from Damogran. Trillian wasn't anybody in particular, or so Zaphod claimed. She just went around with him rather a lot and told him what she thought of him.

"Hi, honey," he said to her.

She flashed him a quick tight smile and looked away. Then she looked back for a moment and smiled more warmly—but by this time he was looking at something else.

"Hi," he said to a small knot of creatures from the press who were standing nearby wishing that he would stop saying *Hi* and get on with the quotes. He grinned at them particularly because he knew that in a few moments he would be giving them one hell of a quote.

The next thing he said though was not a lot of use to them. One of the officials of the party had irritably decided that the President was clearly not in a mood to read the deliciously turned speech that had been written for him, and had flipped the switch on the remote-control device in his pocket. Away in front of them a huge white dome that bulged against the sky cracked down the middle, split and slowly folded itself down into the ground. Everyone gasped although they had known perfectly well it was going to do that because they'd built it that way.

Beneath it lay uncovered a huge starship, one hundred and fifty meters long, shaped like a sleek running shoe, perfectly white and mind-bogglingly beautiful. At the heart of it, unseen, lay a small gold box which carried within it the most brain-wrenching device ever conceived, a device that made this starship unique in the history of the Galaxy, a device after which the ship had been named—the Heart of Gold.

"Wow," said Zaphod Beeblebrox to the Heart of Gold. There wasn't much else he could say.

He said it again because he knew it would annoy the press. "Wow."

The crowd turned their faces back toward him expectantly. He winked at Trillian, who raised her eyebrows and widened her eyes at him. She knew what he was about to say and thought him a terrible show-off.

"That is really amazing," he said. "That really is truly amazing. That is so amazingly amazing I think I'd like to steal it."

A marvelous presidential quote, absolutely true to form. The crowd laughed appreciatively, the newsmen gleefully punched buttons on their Sub-Etha News-Matics and the President grinned.

As he grinned his heart screamed unbearably and he fingered the small Paralyso-Matic bomb that nestled quietly in his pocket.

Finally he could bear it no more. He lifted his heads up to the sky, let out a wild whoop in major thirds, threw the bomb to the ground and ran forward through the sea of suddenly frozen beaming smiles.

Chapter 5

Prostetnic Vogon Jeltz was not a pleasant sight, even for other Vogons. His highly domed nose rose high above a small piggy forehead. His dark green rubbery skin was thick enough for him to play the game of Vogon Civil Service politics, and play it well, and waterproof enough for him to survive indefinitely at sea depths of down to a thousand feet with no ill effects.

Not that he ever went swimming of course. His busy schedule would not allow it. He was the way he was because billions of years ago when the Vogons had first crawled out of the sluggish primeval seas of Vogsphere, and had lain panting and heaving on the planet's virgin shores . . . when the first rays of the bright young Vogsol sun had shone across them that morning, it was as if the forces of evolution had simply given up on them there and then, had turned aside in disgust and written them off as an ugly and unfortunate mistake. They never evolved again: they should never have survived.

The fact that they did is some kind of tribute to the thick-willed slug-brained stubbornness of these creatures. *Evolution?* they said to themselves, *Who needs it?*, and what nature refused to do for them they simply did without until such time as they were able to rectify the gross anatomical inconveniences with surgery.

Meanwhile, the natural forces on the planet Vogsphere had been working overtime to make up for their earlier blunder. They brought forth scintillating jeweled scuttling crabs, which the Vogons ate, smashing their shells with iron mallets; tall aspiring trees of breathtaking slenderness and color which the Vogons cut down and burned the crabmeat with; elegant gazellelike creatures with silken coats and dewy eyes which the Vogons would catch and sit on. They were no use as transport because their backs would snap instantly, but the Vogons sat on them anyway.

Thus the planet Vogsphere whiled away the unhappy millennia until the Vogons suddenly discovered the principles of interstellar travel. Within a few short Vog years every last Vogon had migrated to the Megabrantis cluster, the political hub of the Galaxy, and now formed the immensely powerful backbone of the Galactic Civil Service. They have attempted to acquire learning, they have attempted to acquire style and social graces, but in most respects the modern Vogon is little different from his primitive forebears. Every year they import twenty-seven thousand scintillating jeweled scuttling crabs from their native planet and while away a happy drunken night smashing them to bits with iron mallets.

Prostetnic Vogon Jeltz was a fairly typical Vogon in that he was thoroughly vile. Also, he did not like hitchhikers.

Somewhere in a small dark cabin buried deep in the intestines of Prostetnic Vogon Jeltz's flagship, a small match flared nervously. The owner of the match was not a Vogon, but he knew all about them and was right to be nervous. His name was Ford Prefect.*

He looked about the cabin but could see very little; strange monstrous shadows loomed and leaped with the tiny flickering flame, but all was quiet. He breathed a silent thank you to the Dentrassis. The Dentrassis are an unruly tribe of gourmands, a wild but pleasant bunch whom the Vogons had recently taken to employing as catering staff on their long-haul fleets, on the strict understanding that they keep themselves very much to themselves.

This suited the Dentrassis fine, because they loved Vogon money, which is one of the hardest currencies in space, but loathed the Vogons themselves. The only sort of Vogon a Dentrassi liked to see was an annoyed Vogon.

It was because of this tiny piece of information that Ford Prefect was not now a whiff of hydrogen, ozone and carbon monoxide.

* Ford Prefect's original name is only pronounceable in an obscure Betelgeusian dialect, now virtually extinct since the Great Collapsing Hrung Disaster of Gal./ Sid./Year 03758 which wiped out all the old Praxibetel communities on Betelgeuse Seven. Ford's father was the only man on the entire planet to survive the Great Collapsing Hrung Disaster, by an extraordinary coincidence that he was never able satisfactorily to explain. The whole episode is shrouded in deep mystery: in fact no one ever knew what a Hrung was nor why it had chosen to collapse on Betelgeuse Seven particularly. Ford's father, magnanimously waving aside the clouds of suspicion that had inevitably settled around him, came to live on Betelgeuse Five, where he both fathered and uncled Ford; in memory of his now dead race he christened him in the ancient Praxibetel tongue.

Because Ford never learned to say his original name, his father eventually died of shame, which is still a terminal disease in some parts of the Galaxy. The other kids at school nicknamed him Ix, which in the language of Betelgeuse Five translates as "boy who is not able satisfactorily to explain what a Hrung is, nor why it should choose to collapse on Betelgeuse Seven."

He heard a slight groan. By the light of the match he saw a heavy shape moving slightly on the floor. Quickly he shook the match out, reached in his pocket, found what he was looking for and took it out. He ripped it open and shook it. He crouched on the floor. The shape moved again.

Ford Prefect said, "I bought some peanuts."

Arthur Dent moved, and groaned again, muttering incoherently.

"Here, have some," urged Ford, shaking the packet again, "if you've never been through a matter transference beam before you've probably lost some salt and protein. The beer you had should have cushioned your system a bit."

"Whhhrrr . . ." said Arthur Dent. He opened his eyes. "It's dark," he said.

"Yes," said Ford Prefect, "it's dark."

"No light," said Arthur Dent. "Dark, no light."

One of the things Ford Prefect had always found hardest to understand about humans was their habit of continually stating and repeating the very very obvious, as in *It's a nice day*, or *You're very tall*, or *Oh dear you seem to have fallen down a thirty-foot well, are you all right?* At first Ford had formed a theory to account for this strange behavior. If human beings don't keep exercising their lips, he thought, their mouths probably seize up. After a few months' consideration and observation he abandoned this theory in favor of a new one. If they don't keep on exercising their lips, he thought, their brains start working. After a while he abandoned this one as well as being obstructively cynical and decided he quite liked human beings after all, but he always remained desperately worried abut the terrible number of things they didn't know about.

"Yes," he agreed with Arthur, "no light." He helped Arthur to some peanuts. "How do you feel?" he asked him.

"Like a military academy," said Arthur, "bits of me keep on passing out."

Ford stared at him blankly in the darkness.

"If I asked you where the hell we were," said Arthur weakly, "would I regret it?"

Ford stood up. "We're safe," he said.

"Oh good," said Arthur.

"We're in a small galley cabin," said Ford, "in one of the spaceships of the Vogon Constructor Fleet."

"Ah," said Arthur, "this is obviously some strange usage of the word *safe* that I wasn't previously aware of."

Ford struck another match to help him search for a light switch. Monstrous shadows leaped and loomed again. Arthur struggled to his feet and hugged himself apprehensively. Hideous alien shapes seemed to throng about him, the air was thick with musty smells which sidled into his lungs without identifying themselves, and a low irritating hum kept his brain from focusing.

"How did we get here?" he asked, shivering slightly.

"We hitched a lift," said Ford.

"Excuse me?" said Arthur. "Are you trying to tell me that we just stuck out our thumbs and some green bug-eyed monster stuck his head out and said, 'Hi fellas, hop right in, I can take you as far as the Basingstoke roundabout?'"

"Well," said Ford, "the Thumb's an electronic sub-etha

signaling device, the roundabout's at Barnard's Star six light-years away, but otherwise, that's more or less right."

"And the bug-eyed monster?"

"Is green, yes."

"Fine," said Arthur, "when can I go home?"

"You can't," said Ford Prefect, and found the light switch.

"Shade your eyes . . ." he said, and turned it on.

Even Ford was surprised.

"Good grief," said Arthur, "is this really the interior of a flying saucer?"

Prostetnic Vogon Jeltz heaved his unpleasant green body round the control bridge. He always felt vaguely irritable after demolishing populated planets. He wished that someone would come and tell him that it was all wrong so that he could shout at them and feel better. He flopped as heavily as he could onto his control seat in the hope that it would break and give him something to be genuinely angry about, but it only gave a complaining sort of creak.

"Go away!" he shouted at a young Vogon guard who entered the bridge at that moment. The guard vanished immediately, feeling rather relieved. He was glad it wouldn't now be him who delivered the report they'd just received. The report was an official release which said that a wonderful new form of spaceship drive was at this moment being unveiled at a Government research base on Damogran which would henceforth make all hyperspatial express routes unnecessary.

Another door slid open, but this time the Vogon captain

didn't shout because it was the door from the galley quarters where the Dentrassis prepared his meals. A meal would be most welcome.

A huge furry creature bounded through the door with his lunch tray. It was grinning like a maniac.

Prostetnic Vogon Jeltz was delighted. He knew that when a Dentrassi looked that pleased with itself there was something going on somewhere on the ship that he could get very angry indeed about.

Ford and Arthur stared around them.

"Well, what do you think?" said Ford.

"It's a bit squalid, isn't it?"

Ford frowned at the grubby mattresses, unwashed cups and unidentifiable bits of smelly alien underwear that lay around the cramped cabin.

"Well, this is a working ship, you see," said Ford. "These are the Dentrassis' sleeping quarters."

"I thought you said they were called Vogons or something."

"Yes," said Ford, "the Vogons run the ship, the Dentrassis are the cooks; they let us on board."

"I'm confused," said Arthur.

"Here, have a look at this," said Ford. He sat down on one of the mattresses and rummaged about in his satchel. Arthur prodded the mattress nervously and then sat on it himself: in fact he had very little to be nervous about, because all mattresses grown in the swamps of Sqornshellous Zeta are very thoroughly killed and dried before being put to service. Very few have ever come to life again.

Ford handed the book to Arthur.

"What is it?" asked Arthur.

"The Hitchhiker's Guide to the Galaxy. It's a sort of electronic book. It tells you everything you need to know about anything. That's its job."

Arthur turned it over nervously in his hands.

"I like the cover," he said. " 'Don't Panic.' It's the first helpful or intelligible thing anybody's said to me all day."

"I'll show you how it works," said Ford. He snatched it from Arthur, who was still holding it as if it were a two-week-dead lark, and pulled it out of its cover.

"You press this button here, you see, and the screen lights up, giving you the index."

A screen, about three inches by four, lit up and characters began to flicker across the surface.

"You want to know about Vogons, so I entered that name so." His fingers tapped some more keys. "And there we are."

The words *Vogon Constructor Fleets* flared in green across the screen.

Ford pressed a large red button at the bottom of the screen and words began to undulate across it. At the same time, the book began to speak the entry as well in a still, quiet, measured voice. This is what the book said:

"Vogon Constructor Fleets. Here is what to do if you want to get a lift from a Vogon: forget it. They are one of the most unpleasant races in the Galaxy—not actually evil, but bad-tempered, bureaucratic, officious and callous. They wouldn't even lift a finger to save their own grandmothers from the Ravenous Bugblatter Beast of Traal without orders signed in trip-

licate, sent in, sent back, queried, lost, found, subjected to public inquiry, lost again, and finally buried in soft peat for three months and recycled as firelighters.

"The best way to get a drink out of a Vogon is to stick your finger down his throat, and the best way to irritate him is to feed his grandmother to the Ravenous Bugblatter Beast of Traal.

"On no account allow a Vogon to read poetry at you."

Arthur blinked at it.

"What a strange book. How did we get a lift then?"

"That's the point, it's out of date now," said Ford, sliding the book back into its cover. "I'm doing the field research for the new revised edition, and one of the things I'll have to do is include a bit about how the Vogons now employ Dentrassi cooks, which gives us a rather useful little loophole."

A pained expression crossed Arthur's face. "But who are the Dentrassis?" he said.

"Great guys," said Ford. "They're *the* best cooks and the best drink mixers and they don't give a wet slap about anything else. And they'll always help hitchhikers aboard, partly because they like the company, but mostly because it annoys the Vogons. Which is exactly the sort of thing you need to know if you're an impoverished hitchhiker trying to see the marvels of the Universe for less than thirty Altairian dollars a day. And that's my job. Fun, isn't it?"

Arthur looked lost.

"It's amazing," he said, and frowned at one of the other mattresses.

"Unfortunately I got stuck on the Earth for rather longer than I intended," said Ford. "I came for a week and got stuck for fifteen years."

"But how did you get there in the first place then?"

"Easy, I got a lift with a teaser."

"A teaser?"

"Yeah."

"Er, what is . . ."

"A teaser? Teasers are usually rich kids with nothing to do. They cruise around looking for planets that haven't made interstellar contact yet and buzz them."

"Buzz them?" Arthur began to feel that Ford was enjoying making life difficult for him.

"Yeah," said Ford, "they buzz them. They find some isolated spot with very few people around, then land right by some poor unsuspecting soul whom no one's ever going to believe and then strut up and down in front of him wearing silly antennas on their head and making *beep beep* noises. Rather childish really." Ford leaned back on the mattress with his hands behind his head and looked infuriatingly pleased with himself.

"Ford," insisted Arthur, "I don't know if this sounds like a silly question, but what am I doing here?"

"Well, you know that," said Ford. "I rescued you from the Earth."

"And what's happened to the Earth?"

"Ah. It's been demolished."

"Has it," said Arthur levelly.

"Yes. It just boiled away into space."

"Look," said Arthur, "I'm a bit upset about that."

Ford frowned to himself and seemed to roll the thought around his mind.

"Yes, I can understand that," he said at last.

"Understand that!" shouted Arthur. "Understand that!"

Ford sprang up.

"Keep looking at the book!" he hissed urgently.

"What?"

"Don't Panic."

"I'm not panicking!"

"Yes, you are."

"All right, so I'm panicking, what else is there to do?"

"You just come along with me and have a good time. The Galaxy's a fun place. You'll need to have this fish in your ear."

"I beg your pardon?" asked Arthur, rather politely he thought.

Ford was holding up a small glass jar which quite clearly had a small yellow fish wriggling around in it. Arthur blinked at him. He wished there was something simple and recognizable he could grasp hold of. He would have felt safe if alongside the Dentrassis' underwear, the piles of Sqorn-shellous mattresses and the man from Betelgeuse holding up a small yellow fish and offering to put it in his ear he had been able to see just a small packet of cornflakes. But he couldn't, and he didn't feel safe.

Suddenly a violent noise leaped at them from no source that he could identify. He gasped in terror at what sounded like a man trying to gargle while fighting off a pack of wolves.

"Shush!" said Ford. "Listen, it might be important."

"Im . . . important?"

"It's the Vogon captain making an announcement on the tannoy."

"You mean that's how the Vogons talk?"

"Listen!"

"But I can't speak Vogon!"

"You don't need to. Just put this fish in your ear."

Ford, with a lightning movement, clapped his hand to Arthur's ear, and he had the sudden sickening sensation of the fish slithering deep into his aural tract. Gasping with horror he scrabbled at his ear for a second or so, but then slowly turned goggle-eyed with wonder. He was experiencing the aural equivalent of looking at a picture of two black silhouetted faces and suddenly seeing it as a picture of a white candlestick. Or of looking at a lot of colored dots on a piece of paper which suddenly resolve themselves into the figure six and mean that your optician is going to charge you a lot of money for a new pair of glasses.

He was still listening to the howling gargles, he knew that, only now it had somehow taken on the semblance of perfectly straightforward English.

This is what he heard . . .

Chapter 6

Howl *howl gargle howl gargle howl howl howl gargle howl gargle howl howl gargle gargle howl gargle gargle gargle howl slurrp uuuurgh* should have a good time. Message repeats. This is your captain speaking, so stop whatever you're doing and pay attention. First of all I see from our instruments that we have a couple of hitchhikers aboard. Hello, wherever you are. I just want to make it totally clear that you are not at all welcome. I worked hard to get where I am today, and I didn't become captain of a Vogon constructor ship simply so I could turn it into a taxi service for a load of degenerate freeloaders. I have sent out a search party, and as soon as they find you I will put you off the ship. If you're very lucky I might read you some of my poetry first.

"Secondly, we are about to jump into hyperspace for the journey to Barnard's Star. On arrival we will stay in dock for a seventy-two-hour refit, and no one's to leave the ship during that time. I repeat, all planet leave is canceled. I've just had an unhappy love affair, so I don't see why anybody else should have a good time. Message ends."

The noise stopped.

Arthur discovered to his embarrassment that he was lying curled up in a small ball on the floor with his arms wrapped round his head. He smiled weakly.

"Charming man," he said. "I wish I had a daughter so I could forbid her to marry one . . ."

"You wouldn't need to," said Ford. "They've got as much sex appeal as a road accident. No, don't move," he added as Arthur began to uncurl himself, "you'd better be prepared for the jump into hyperspace. It's unpleasantly like being drunk."

"What's so unpleasant about being drunk?"

"You ask a glass of water."

Arthur thought about this.

"Ford," he said.

"Yeah?"

"What's this fish doing in my ear?"

"It's translating for you. It's a Babel fish. Look it up in the book if you like."

He tossed over *The Hitchhiker's Guide to the Galaxy* and then curled himself up into a fetal ball to prepare himself for the jump.

At that moment the bottom fell out of Arthur's mind.

His eyes turned inside out. His feet began to leak out of the top of his head.

The room folded flat around him, spun around, shifted out of existence and left him sliding into his own navel.

They were passing through hyperspace.

"The Babel fish," said *The Hitchhiker's Guide to the Galaxy* quietly, *"is small, yellow and leechlike, and probably the oddest thing in the Universe. It feeds on brainwave energy received not from its own carrier but from those around it. It absorbs all unconscious mental frequencies from this brainwave energy to nourish itself with. It then excretes into the mind of*

its carrier a telepathic matrix formed by combining the conscious thought frequencies with nerve signals picked up from the speech centers of the brain which has supplied them. The practical upshot of all this is that if you stick a Babel fish in your ear you can instantly understand anything said to you in any form of language. The speech patterns you actually hear decode the brainwave matrix which has been fed into your mind by your Babel fish.

"Now it is such a bizarrely improbable coincidence that anything so mind-bogglingly useful could have evolved purely by chance that some thinkers have chosen to see it as a final and clinching proof of the nonexistence of God.

"The argument goes something like this: 'I refuse to prove that I exist,' says God, 'for proof denies faith, and without faith I am nothing.'

" 'But,' says Man, 'the Babel fish is a dead giveaway, isn't it? It could not have evolved by chance. It proves you exist, and so therefore, by your own arguments, you don't. QED.'

" 'Oh dear,' says God, 'I hadn't thought of that,' and promptly vanishes in a puff of logic.

" 'Oh, that was easy,' says Man, and for an encore goes on to prove that black is white and gets himself killed on the next pedestrian crossing.

"Most leading theologians claim that this argument is a load of dingo's kidneys, but that didn't stop Oolon Colluphid making a small fortune when he used it as the central theme of his best-selling book, Well That about Wraps It Up for God.

"Meanwhile, the poor Babel fish, by effectively removing all barriers to communication between different races and cul-

tures, has caused more and bloodier wars than anything else in the history of creation."

Arthur let out a low groan. He was horrified to discover that the kick through hyperspace hadn't killed him. He was now six light-years from the place that the Earth would have been if it still existed.

The Earth.

Visions of it swam sickeningly through his nauseated mind. There was no way his imagination could feel the impact of the whole Earth having gone, it was too big. He prodded his feelings by thinking that his parents and his sister had gone. No reaction. He thought of all the people he had been close to. No reaction. Then he thought of a complete stranger he had been standing behind in the queue at the supermarket two days before and felt a sudden stab— the supermarket was gone, everyone in it was gone. Nelson's Column had gone! Nelson's Column had gone and there would be no outcry, because there was no one left to make an outcry. From now on Nelson's Column only existed in his mind. England only existed in his mind—his mind, stuck here in this dank smelly steel-lined spaceship. A wave of claustrophobia closed in on him.

England no longer existed. He'd got that—somehow he'd got it. He tried again. America, he thought, has gone. He couldn't grasp it. He decided to start smaller again. New York has gone. No reaction. He'd never seriously believed it existed anyway. The dollar, he thought, has sunk for ever. Slight tremor there. Every Bogart movie has been wiped, he said to himself, and that gave him a nasty knock.

McDonald's, he thought. There is no longer any such thing as a McDonald's hamburger.

He passed out. When he came round a second later he found he was sobbing for his mother.

He jerked himself violently to his feet.

"Ford!"

Ford looked up from where he was sitting in a corner humming to himself. He always found the actual traveling-through-space part of space travel rather trying.

"Yeah?" he said.

"If you're a researcher on this book thing and you were on Earth, you must have been gathering material on it."

"Well, I was able to extend the original entry a bit, yes."

"Let me see what it says in this edition then, I've got to see it."

"Yeah, okay." He passed it over again.

Arthur grabbed hold of it and tried to stop his hands shaking. He pressed the entry for the relevant page. The screen flashed and swirled and resolved into a page of print. Arthur stared at it.

"It doesn't have an entry!" he burst out.

Ford looked over his shoulder.

"Yes, it does," he said, "down there, see at the bottom of the screen, just above Eccentrica Gallumbits, the triple-breasted whore of Eroticon 6."

Arthur followed Ford's finger, and saw where it was pointing. For a moment it still didn't register, then his mind nearly blew up.

"What? *Harmless?* Is that all it's got to say? *Harmless!* One word!"

Ford shrugged.

"Well, there are a hundred billion stars in the Galaxy, and only a limited amount of space in the book's microprocessors," he said, "and no one knew much about the Earth, of course."

"Well, for God's sake, I hope you managed to rectify that a bit."

"Oh yes, well, I managed to transmit a new entry off to the editor. He had to trim it a bit, but it's still an improvement."

"And what does it say now?" asked Arthur.

"Mostly harmless," admitted Ford with a slightly embarrassed cough.

"Mostly harmless!" shouted Arthur.

"What was that noise?" hissed Ford.

"It was me shouting," shouted Arthur.

"No! Shut up!" said Ford. "I think we're in trouble."

"You think we're in trouble!"

Outside the door were the clear sounds of marching footsteps.

"The Dentrassis?" whispered Arthur.

"No, those are steel-tipped boots," said Ford.

There was a sharp ringing rap on the door.

"Then who is it?" said Arthur.

"Well," said Ford, "if we're lucky it's just the Vogons come to throw us in to space."

"And if we're unlucky?"

"If we're unlucky," said Ford grimly, "the captain might be serious in his threat that he's going to read us some of his poetry first. . . ."

Chapter 7

Vogon poetry is of course the third worst in the Universe. The second worst is that of the Azgoths of Kria. During a recitation by their Poet Master Grunthos the Flatulent of his poem "Ode to a Small Lump of Green Putty I Found in My Armpit One Midsummer Morning" four of his audience died of internal hemorrhaging, and the President of the Mid-Galactic Arts Nobbling Council survived by gnawing one of his own legs off. Grunthos is reported to have been "disappointed" by the poem's reception, and was about to embark on a reading of his twelve-book epic entitled *My Favorite Bathtime Gurgles* when his own major intestine, in a desperate attempt to save life and civilization, leaped straight up through his neck and throttled his brain.

The very worst poetry of all perished along with its creator, Paula Nancy Millstone Jennings of Greenbridge, Essex, England, in the destruction of the planet Earth.

Prostetnic Vogon Jeltz smiled very slowly. This was done not so much for effect as because he was trying to remember the sequence of muscle movements. He had had a terribly therapeutic yell at his prisoners and was now feeling quite relaxed and ready for a little callousness.

The prisoners sat in Poetry Appreciation chairs—strapped in. Vogons suffered no illusions as to the regard their works were generally held in. Their early attempts at composition had been part of a bludgeoning insistence that they be accepted as a properly evolved and cultured race, but now the only thing that kept them going was sheer bloody-mindedness.

The sweat stood out cold on Ford Prefect's brow, and slid round the electrodes strapped to his temples. These were attached to a battery of electronic equipment—imagery intensifiers, rhythmic modulators, alliterative residulators and simile dumpers—all designed to heighten the experience of the poem and make sure that not a single nuance of the poet's thought was lost.

Arthur Dent sat and quivered. He had no idea what he was in for, but he knew that he hadn't liked anything that had happened so far and didn't think things were likely to change.

The Vogon began to read—a fetid little passage of his own devising.

"*Oh freddled gruntbuggly . . .*" he began. Spasms wracked Ford's body—this was worse than even he'd been prepared for.

"*? . . . thy micturations are to me/ As plurdled gabbleblotchits on a lurgid bee.*"

"Aaaaaaarggggghhhhhh!" went Ford Prefect, wrenching his head back as lumps of pain thumped through it. He could dimly see beside him Arthur lolling and rolling in his seat. He clenched his teeth.

"*Groop I implore thee,*" continued the merciless Vogon, "*my foonting turlingdromes.*"

His voice was rising to a horrible pitch of impassioned

stridency. *"And hooptiously drangle me with crinkly bind-lewurdles,/ Or I will rend thee in the gobberwarts with my blurglecruncheon, see if I don't!"*

"Nnnnnnnnnnnyyyyyyyyuuuuuuurrrrrrrggggggghhhhh!" cried Ford Prefect and threw one final spasm as the electronic enhancement of the last line caught him full blast across the temples. He went limp.

Arthur lolled.

"Now, Earthlings . . ." whirred the Vogon (he didn't know that Ford Prefect was in fact from a small planet somewhere in the vicinity of Betelgeuse, and wouldn't have cared if he had), "I present you with a simple choice! Either die in the vacuum of space, or . . ." he paused for melodramatic effect, "tell me how good you thought my poem was!"

He threw himself backward into a huge leathery bat-shaped seat and watched them. He did the smile again.

Ford was rasping for breath. He rolled his dusty tongue round his parched mouth and moaned.

Arthur said brightly, "Actually I quite liked it."

Ford turned and gaped. Here was an approach that had quite simply not occurred to him.

The Vogon raised a surprised eyebrow that effectively obscured his nose and was therefore no bad thing.

"Oh good . . ." he whirred, in considerable astonishment.

"Oh yes," said Arthur, "I thought that some of the metaphysical imagery was really particularly effective."

Ford continued to stare at him, slowly organizing his thoughts around this totally new concept. Were they really going to be able to bareface their way out of this?

"Yes, do continue . . ." invited the Vogon.

"Oh . . . and, er . . . interesting rhythmic devices too," continued Arthur, "which seemed to counterpoint the . . . er . . . er . . ." he floundered.

Ford leaped to his rescue, hazarding ". . . counterpoint the surrealism of the underlying metaphor of the . . . er . . ." He floundered too, but Arthur was ready again.

". . . humanity of the . . ."

"*Vogonity*," Ford hissed at him.

"Ah yes, Vogonity—sorry—of the poet's compassionate soul"—Arthur felt he was on a homestretch now—"which contrives through the medium of the verse structure to sublimate this, transcend that, and come to terms with the fundamental dichotomies of the other"—he was reaching a triumphant crescendo—"and one is left with a profound and vivid insight into . . . into . . . er . . ." (which suddenly gave out on him). Ford leaped in with the coup de grace:

"Into whatever it was the poem was about!" he yelled. Out of the corner of his mouth: "Well done, Arthur, that was very good."

The Vogon perused them. For a moment his embittered racial soul had been touched, but he thought no—too little too late. His voice took on the quality of a cat snagging brushed nylon.

"So what you're saying is that I write poetry because underneath my mean callous heartless exterior I really just want to be loved," he said. He paused, "Is that right?"

Ford laughed a nervous laugh. "Well, I mean, yes," he said, "don't we all, deep down, you know . . . er . . ."

The Vogon stood up.

"No, well, you're completely wrong," he said, "I just write poetry to throw my mean callous heartless exterior into sharp relief. I'm going to throw you off the ship anyway. Guard! Take the prisoners to number three airlock and throw them out!"

"What?" shouted Ford.

A huge young Vogon guard stepped forward and yanked them out of their straps with his huge blubbery arms.

"You can't throw us into space," yelled Ford, "we're trying to write a book."

"Resistance is useless!" shouted the Vogon guard back at him. It was the first phrase he'd learned when he joined the Vogon Guard Corps.

The captain watched with detached amusement and then turned away.

Arthur stared round him wildly.

"I don't want to die now!" he yelled. "I've still got a headache! I don't want to go to heaven with a headache, I'd be all cross and wouldn't enjoy it!"

The guard grasped them both firmly round the neck, and bowing deferentially toward his captain's back, hoicked them both protesting out of the bridge. A steel door closed and the captain was on his own again. He hummed quietly and mused to himself, lightly fingering his notebook of verses.

"Hmmm," he said, *counterpoint the surrealism of the underlying metaphor. . . ."* He considered this for a moment, and then closed the book with a grim smile.

"Death's too good for them," he said.

The long steel-lined corridor echoed to the feeble struggles of the two humanoids clamped firmly under rubbery Vogon armpits.

"This is great," spluttered Arthur, "this is really terrific. Let go of me, you brute!"

The Vogon guard dragged them on.

"Don't you worry," said Ford, "I'll think of something." He didn't sound hopeful.

"Resistance is useless!" bellowed the guard.

"Just don't say things like that," stammered Ford. "How can anyone maintain a positive mental attitude if you're saying things like that?"

"My God," complained Arthur, "you're talking about a positive mental attitude and you haven't even had your planet demolished today. I woke up this morning and thought I'd have a nice relaxed day, do a bit of reading, brush the dog. . . . It's now just after four in the afternoon and I'm already being thrown out of an alien spaceship six light-years from the smoking remains of the Earth!" He spluttered and gurgled as the Vogon tightened his grip.

"All right," said Ford, "just stop panicking!"

"Who said anything about panicking?" snapped Arthur. "This is still just the culture shock. You wait till I've settled down into the situation and found my bearings. *Then* I'll start panicking!"

"Arthur, you're getting hysterical. Shut up!" Ford tried desperately to think, but was interrupted by the guard shouting again.

"Resistance is useless!"

"And you can shut up as well!" snapped Ford.

"Resistance is useless!"

"Oh, give it a rest," said Ford. He twisted his head till he was looking straight up into his captor's face. A thought struck him.

"Do you really enjoy this sort of thing?" he asked suddenly.

The Vogon stopped dead and a look of immense stupidity seeped slowly over his face.

"Enjoy?" he boomed. "What do you mean?"

"What I mean," said Ford, "is does it give you a full, satisfying life? Stomping around, shouting, pushing people out of spaceships . . ."

The Vogon stared up at the low steel ceiling and his eyebrows almost rolled over each other. His mouth slacked. Finally he said, "Well, the hours are good. . . ."

"They'd have to be," agreed Ford.

Arthur twisted his head round to look at Ford.

"Ford, what are you doing?" he asked in an amazed whisper.

"Oh, just trying to take an interest in the world around me, okay?" he said. "So the hours are pretty good then?" he resumed.

The Vogon stared down at him as sluggish thoughts moiled around in the murky depths.

"Yeah," he said, "but now you come to mention it, most of the actual minutes are pretty lousy. Except . . ." he thought again, which required looking at the ceiling, "except some of the shouting I quite like." He filled his lungs and bellowed, "Resistance is . . ."

"Sure, yes," interrupted Ford hurriedly, "you're good at that, I can tell. But if it's mostly lousy," he said, slowly giving the words time to reach their mark, "then why do you do it? What is it? The girls? The leather? The machismo? Or do you just find that coming to terms with the mindless tedium of it all presents an interesting challenge?"

Arthur looked backward and forward between them in bafflement.

"Er . . ." said the guard, "er . . . er . . . I dunno. I think I just sort of . . . do it really. My aunt said that spaceship guard was a good career for a young Vogon—you know, the uniform, the low-slung stun ray holster, the mindless tedium . . ."

"There you are, Arthur," said Ford with the air of someone reaching the conclusion of his argument, "you think you've got problems."

Arthur rather thought he had. Apart from the unpleasant business with his home planet the Vogon guard had half-throttled him already and he didn't like the sound of being thrown into space very much.

"Try and understand *his* problem," insisted Ford. "Here he is, poor lad, his entire life's work is stamping around, throwing people off spaceships . . ."

"And shouting," added the guard.

"And shouting, sure," said Ford, patting the blubbery arm clamped round his neck in friendly condescension, "and he doesn't even know why he's doing it!"

Arthur agreed this was very sad. He did this with a small feeble gesture, because he was too asphyxiated to speak.

Deep rumblings of bemusement came from the guard.

"Well. Now you put it like that I suppose . . ."

"Good lad!" encouraged Ford.

"But all right," went on the rumblings, "so what's the alternative?"

"Well," said Ford, brightly but slowly, "stop doing it, of

course! Tell them," he went on, "you're not going to do it any more." He felt he ought to add something to that, but for the moment the guard seemed to have his mind occupied pondering that much.

"Eerrrrrmmmmmmmmmmmmmmmmmmmmmmmm . . ." said the guard, "erm, well, that doesn't sound that great to me."

Ford suddenly felt the moment slipping away.

"Now wait a minute," he said, "that's just the start, you see, there's more to it than that, you see. . . ."

But at that moment the guard renewed his grip and continued his original purpose of lugging his prisoners to the airlock. He was obviously quite touched.

"No, I think if it's all the same to you," he said, "I'd better get you both shoved into this airlock and then go and get on with some other bits of shouting I've got to do."

It wasn't all the same to Ford Prefect at all.

"Come on now . . . but look!" he said, less slowly, less brightly.

"Huhhhhggggggggnnnnnnn . . ." said Arthur without any clear inflection.

"But hang on," pursued Ford, "there's music and art and things to tell you about yet! Arrggghhh!"

"Resistance is useless," bellowed the guard, and then added, "You see, if I keep it up I can eventually get promoted to Senior Shouting Officer, and there aren't usually many vacancies for nonshouting and nonpushing-people-about officers, so I think I'd better stick to what I know."

They had now reached the airlock—a large circular steel hatchway of massive strength and weight let into the inner skin of the craft. The guard operated a control and the hatchway swung smoothly open.

"But thanks for taking an interest," said the Vogon guard. "Bye now." He flung Ford and Arthur through the hatchway into the small chamber within. Arthur lay panting for breath. Ford scrambled round and flung his shoulder uselessly against the reclosing hatchway.

"But listen," he shouted to the guard, "there's a whole world you don't know anything about . . . here, how about this?" Desperately he grabbed for the only bit of culture he knew offhand—he hummed the first bar of Beethoven's "Fifth."

"*Da da da dum!* Doesn't that stir anything in you?"

"No," said the guard, "not really. But I'll mention it to my aunt."

If he said anything further after that it was lost. The hatchway sealed itself tight, and all sound was lost except the faint distant hum of the ship's engines.

They were in a brightly polished cylindrical chamber about six feet in diameter and ten feet long.

Ford looked round it, panting.

"Potentially bright lad I thought," he said, and slumped against the curved wall.

Arthur was still lying in the curve of the floor where he had fallen. He didn't look up. He just lay panting.

"We're trapped now, aren't we?"

"Yes," said Ford, "we're trapped."

"Well, didn't you think of anything? I thought you said you were going to think of something. Perhaps you thought of something and I didn't notice."

"Oh yes, I thought of something," panted Ford.

Arthur looked up expectantly.

"But unfortunately," continued Ford, "it rather involved being on the other side of this airtight hatchway." He kicked the hatch they'd just been thrown through.

"But it was a good idea, was it?"

"Oh yes, very neat."

"What was it?"

"Well, I hadn't worked out the details yet. Not much point now, is there?"

"So . . . er, what happens next?" asked Arthur.

"Oh, er, well, the hatchway in front of us will open automatically in a few moments and we will shoot out into deep space I expect and asphyxiate. If you take a lungful of air with you you can last for up to thirty seconds, of course . . ." said Ford. He stuck his hands behind his back, raised his eyebrows and started to hum an old Betelgeusian battle hymn. To Arthur's eyes he suddenly looked very alien.

"So this is it," said Arthur, "we are going to die."

"Yes," said Ford, "except . . . no! Wait a minute!" He suddenly lunged across the chamber at something behind Arthur's line of vision. "What's this switch?" he cried.

"What? Where?" cried Arthur, twisting round.

"No, I was only fooling," said Ford, "we are going to die after all."

He slumped against the wall again and carried on the tune from where he left off.

"You know," said Arthur, "it's at times like this, when I'm trapped in a Vogon airlock with a man from Betelgeuse, and about to die of asphyxiation in deep space, that I really wish I'd listened to what my mother told me when I was young."

"Why, what did she tell you?"

"I don't know, I didn't listen."

"Oh." Ford carried on humming.

"This is terrific," Arthur thought to himself, "Nelson's Column has gone, McDonald's has gone, all that's left is me and the words *Mostly harmless*. Any second now all that will be left is *Mostly harmless*. And yesterday the planet seemed to be going so well."

A motor whirred.

A slight hiss built into a deafening roar of rushing air as the outer hatchway opened onto an empty blackness studded with tiny, impossibly bright points of light. Ford and Arthur popped into outer space like corks from a toy gun.

Chapter 8

The Hitchhiker's Guide to the Galaxy *is a wholly remarkable book. It has been compiled and recompiled many times over many years and under many different editorships. It contains contributions from countless numbers of travelers and researchers.*

The introduction begins like this:

"Space," *it says,* "is big. Really big. You just won't believe how vastly hugely mind-bogglingly big it is. I mean, you may think it's a long way down the road to the chemist, but that's just peanuts to space. Listen . . ." *and so on.*

(After a while the style settles down a bit and it begins to tell you things you really need to know, like the fact that the fabulously beautiful planet Bethselamin is now so worried about the cumulative erosion by ten billion visiting tourists a year that any net imbalance between the amount you eat and the amount you excrete while on the planet is surgically removed from your body weight when you leave: so every time you go to the lavatory there it is vitally important to get a receipt.)

To be fair though, when confronted by the sheer enormity of the distances between the stars, better minds than the one responsible for the Guide's introduction have faltered. Some invite you to consider for a moment a peanut in Reading and a small walnut in Johannesburg, and other such dizzying concepts.

The simple truth is that interstellar distances will not fit into the human imagination.

Even light, which travels so fast that it takes most races thousands of years to realize that it travels at all, takes time to journey between the stars. It takes eight minutes to journey from the star Sol to the place where the Earth used to be, and four years more to arrive at Sol's nearest stellar neighbor, Alpha Proxima.

For light to reach the other side of the Galaxy, for it to reach Damogran, for instance, takes rather longer: five hundred thousand years.

The record for hitchhiking this distance is just under five years, but you don't get to see much on the way.

The Hitchhiker's Guide to the Galaxy *says that if you hold a lungful of air you can survive in the total vacuum of space for about thirty seconds. However, it does go on to say that what with space being the mind-boggling size it is the chances of getting picked up by another ship within those thirty seconds are two to the power of two hundred and seventy-six thousand, seven hundred and nine to one against.*

By a totally staggering coincidence, that is also the telephone number of an Islington flat where Arthur once went to a very good party and met a very nice girl whom he totally failed to get off with—she went off with a gate-crasher.

Though the planet Earth, the Islington flat and the telephone have all now been demolished, it is comforting to reflect that they are all in some small way commemorated by the fact that twenty-nine seconds later Ford and Arthur were rescued.

computer chattered to itself in alarm as it noticed an airlock open and close itself for no apparent reason.

This was because reason was in fact out to lunch.

A hole had just appeared in the Galaxy. It was exactly a nothingth of a second long, a nothingth of an inch wide, and quite a lot of millions of light-years from end to end.

As it closed up, lots of paper hats and party balloons fell out of it and drifted off through the Universe. A team of seven three-foot-high market analysts fell out of it and died, partly of asphyxiation, partly of surprise.

Two hundred and thirty-nine thousand lightly fried eggs fell out of it too, materializing in a large wobbly heap on the famine-struck land of Poghril in the Pansel system.

The whole Poghril tribe had died out from famine except for one last man who died of cholesterol poisoning some weeks later.

The nothingth of a second for which the hole existed reverberated backward and forward through time in a most improbable fashion. Somewhere in the deeply remote past it seriously traumatized a small random group of atoms drifting through the empty sterility of space and made them cling together in the most extraordinarily unlikely patterns.

These patterns quickly learned to copy themselves (this was part of what was so extraordinary about the patterns) and went on to cause massive trouble on every planet they drifted on to. That was how life began in the Universe.

Five wild Event Maelstroms swirled in vicious storms of unreason and spewed up a payment.

On the pavement lay Ford Prefect and Arthur Dent gulping like half-spent fish.

"There you are," gasped Ford, scrabbling for a finger hold on the pavement as it raced through the Third Reach of the Unknown, "I told you I'd think of something."

"Oh sure," said Arthur, "sure."

"Bright idea of mine," said Ford, "to find a passing spaceship and get rescued by it."

The real Universe arched sickeningly away beneath them. Various pretend ones flitted silently by, like mountain goats. Primal light exploded, splattering space-time as with gobbets of Jello-O. Time blossomed, matter shrank away. The highest prime number coalesced quietly in a corner and hid itself away for ever.

"Oh, come off it," said Arthur, "the chances against it were astronomical."

"Don't knock it, it worked," said Ford.

"What sort of ship are we in?" asked Arthur as the pit of eternity yawned beneath them.

"I don't know," said Ford, "I haven't opened my eyes yet."

"No, nor have I," said Arthur.

The Universe jumped, froze, quivered and splayed out in several unexpected directions.

Arthur and Ford opened their eyes and looked about in considerable surprise.

"Good God," said Arthur, "it looks just like the sea front at Southend."

"Hell, I'm relieved to hear you say that," said Ford.

"Why?"

"Because I thought I must be going mad."

"Perhaps you are. Perhaps you only thought I said it."

Ford thought about this.

"Well, did you say it or didn't you?" he asked.

"I think so," said Arthur.

"Well, perhaps we're both going mad."

"Yes," said Arthur, "we'd be mad, all things considered, to think this was Southend."

"Well, do you think this is Southend?"

"Oh yes."

"So do I."

"Therefore we must be mad."

"Nice day for it."

"Yes," said a passing maniac.

"Who was that?" asked Arthur.

"Who—the man with the five heads and the elderberry bush full of kippers?"

"Yes."

"I don't know. Just someone."

"Ah."

They both sat on the pavement and watched with a certain unease as huge children bounced heavily along the sand and wild horses thundered through the sky taking fresh supplies of reinforced railings to the Uncertain Areas.

"You know," said Arthur with a slight cough, "if this is Southend, there's something very odd about it. . . ."

"You mean the way the sea stays steady as a rock and the buildings keep washing up and down?" said Ford. "Yes, I thought that was odd too. In fact," he continued as with a huge bang Southend split itself into six equal segments which danced and spun giddily round each other in lewd and licentious formations, "there is something altogether very strange going on."

Wild yowling noises of pipes and strings seared through the wind, hot doughnuts popped out of the road for ten pence each, horrid fish stormed out of the sky and Arthur and Ford decided to make a run for it.

They plunged through heavy walls of sound, mountains of archaic thought, valleys of mood music, bad shoe sessions and footling bats and suddenly heard a girl's voice.

It sounded quite a sensible voice, but it just said, "Two to the power of one hundred thousand to one against and falling," and that was all.

Ford skidded down a beam of light and spun round trying to find a source for the voice but could see nothing he could seriously believe in.

"What was that voice?" shouted Arthur.

"I don't know," yelled Ford, "I don't know. It sounded like a measurement of probability."

"Probability? What do you mean?"

"Probability. You know, like two to one, three to one, five to four against. It said two to the power of one hundred thousand to one against. That's pretty improbable, you know."

A million-gallon vat of custard upended itself over them without warning.

"But what does it mean?" cried Arthur.

"What, the custard?"

"No, the measurement of improbability!"

"I don't know. I don't know at all. I think we're on some kind of spaceship."

"I can only assume," said Arthur, "that this is not the first-class compartment."

Bulges appeared in the fabric of space-time. Great ugly bulges.

"Haaaauuurrgghhh . . ." said Arthur, as he felt his body softening and bending in unusual directions. "Southend seems to be melting away . . . the stars are swirling . . . a dustbowl . . . my legs are drifting off into the sunset . . . my left arm's come off too." A frightening thought struck him. "Hell," he said, "how am I going to operate my digital watch now?" He wound his eyes desperately around in Ford's direction.

"Ford," he said, "you're turning into a penguin. Stop it."

Again came the voice.

"Two to the power of seventy-five thousand to one against and falling."

Ford waddled around his pond in a furious circle.

"Hey, who are you?" he quacked. "Where are you? What's going on and is there any way of stopping it?"

"Please relax," said the voice pleasantly, like a stewardess in an airliner with only one wing and two engines, one of which is on fire, "you are perfectly safe."

"But that's not the point!" raged Ford. "The point is that

I am now a perfectly safe penguin, and my colleague here is rapidly running out of limbs!"

"It's all right, I've got them back now," said Arthur.

"Two to the power of fifty thousand to one against and falling," said the voice.

"Admittedly," said Arthur, "they're longer than I usually like them, but . . ."

"Isn't there anything," squawked Ford in avian fury, "you feel you ought to be telling us?"

The voice cleared its throat. A giant petit four lolloped off into the distance.

"Welcome," the voice said, "to the Starship Heart of Gold."

The voice continued.

"Please do not be alarmed," it said, "by anything you see or hear around you. You are bound to feel some initial ill effects as you have been rescued from certain death at an improbability level of two to the power of two hundred and seventy-six thousand to one against—possibly much higher. We are now cruising at a level of two to the power of twenty-five thousand to one against and falling, and we will be restoring normality just as soon as we are sure what is normal anyway. Thank you. Two to the power of twenty thousand to one against and falling."

The voice cut out.

Ford and Arthur were in a small luminous pink cubicle.

Ford was wildly excited.

"Arthur!" he said, "this is fantastic! We've been picked up by a ship powered by the Infinite Improbability Drive!

This is incredible! I heard rumors about it before! They were all officially denied, but they must have done it! They've built the Improbability Drive! Arthur, this is . . . Arthur? What's happening?"

Arthur had jammed himself against the door to the cubicle, trying to hold it closed, but it was ill fitting. Tiny furry little hands were squeezing themselves through the cracks, their fingers were ink-stained; tiny voices chattered insanely.

Arthur looked up.

"Ford!" he said, "there's an infinite number of monkeys outside who want to talk to us about this script for *Hamlet* they've worked out."

Chapter 10

The Infinite Improbability Drive is a wonderful new method of crossing vast interstellar distances in a mere nothingth of a second, without all that tedious mucking about in hyperspace.

It was discovered by a lucky chance, and then developed into a governable form of propulsion by the Galactic Government's research team on Damogran.

This, briefly, is the story of its discovery.

The principle of generating small amounts of *finite* improbability by simply hooking the logic circuits of a Bambleweeny 57 Sub-Meson Brain to an atomic vector plotter suspended in a strong Brownian Motion producer (say a nice hot cup of tea) were of course well understood—and such generators were often used to break the ice at parties by making all the molecules in the hostess's undergarments leap simultaneously one foot to the left, in accordance with the Theory of Indeterminacy.

Many respectable physicists said that they weren't going to stand for this, partly because it was a debasement of science, but mostly because they didn't get invited to those sorts of parties.

Another thing they couldn't stand was the perpetual failure they encountered in trying to construct a machine which could generate the *infinite* improbability field needed to flip a spaceship across the mind-paralyzing distances between the farthest stars, and in the end they grumpily announced that such a machine was virtually impossible.

Then, one day, a student who had been left to sweep up the lab after a particularly unsuccessful party found himself reasoning this way:

If, he thought to himself, such a machine is a *virtual* impossibility, then it must logically be a *finite* improbability. So all I have to do in order to make one is to work out exactly how improbable it is, feed that figure into the finite improbability generator, give it a fresh cup of really hot tea . . . and turn it on!

He did this, and was rather startled to discover that he had managed to create the long-sought-after golden Infinite Improbability generator out of thin air.

It startled him even more when just after he was awarded the Galactic Institute's Prize for Extreme Cleverness he got lynched by a rampaging mob of respectable physicists who had finally realized that the one thing they really couldn't stand was a smart-ass.

Chapter 11

The improbability-proof control cabin of the Heart of Gold looked like a perfectly conventional spaceship except that it was perfectly clean because it was so new. Some of the control seats hadn't had the plastic wrapping taken off yet. The cabin was mostly white, oblong, and about the size of a smallish restaurant. In fact it wasn't perfectly oblong: the two long walls were raked round in a slight parallel curve, and all the angles and corners of the cabin were contoured in excitingly chunky shapes. The truth of the matter is that it would have been a great deal simpler and more practical to build the cabin as an ordinary three-dimensional oblong room, but then the designers would have got miserable. As it was the cabin looked excitingly purposeful, with large video screens ranged over the control and guidance system panels on the concave wall, and long banks of computers set into the convex wall. In one corner a robot sat humped, its gleaming brushed steel head hanging loosely between its gleaming brushed steel knees. It too was fairly new, but though it was beautifully constructed and polished it somehow looked as if the various parts of its more or less humanoid body didn't quite fit properly. In fact they fitted perfectly well, but something in its bearing suggested that they might have fitted better.

Zaphod Beeblebrox paced nervously up and down the cabin, brushing his hands over pieces of gleaming equipment and giggling with excitement.

Trillian sat hunched over a clump of instruments reading off figures. Her voice was carried round the tannoy system of the whole ship.

"Five to one against and falling . . ." she said, *"four to one against and falling . . . three to one . . . two . . . one . . . probability factor of one to one . . . we have normality, I repeat we have normality."* She turned her microphone off—then turned it back on—with a slight smile and continued: *"Anything you still can't cope with is therefore your own problem. Please relax. You will be sent for soon."*

Zaphod burst out in annoyance, "Who are they, Trillian?"

Trillian spun her seat round to face him and shrugged.

"Just a couple of guys we seem to have picked up in open space," she said. "Section ZZ$_9$ Plural Z Alpha."

"Yeah, well, that's a very sweet thought, Trillian," complained Zaphod, "but do you really think it's wise under the circumstances? I mean, here we are on the run and everything, we must have the police of half the Galaxy after us by now, and we stop to pick up hitchhikers. Okay, so ten out of ten for style, but minus several million for good thinking, yeah?"

He tapped irritably at a control panel. Trillian quietly moved his hand before he tapped anything important. Whatever Zaphod's qualities of mind might include—dash, bravado, conceit—he was mechanically inept and could easily blow the ship up with an extravagant guesture. Trillian had come to suspect that the main reason he had had such a wild and successful life was that he never really understood the significance of anything he did.

"Zaphod," she said patiently, "they were floating unprotected in open space . . . you wouldn't want them to have died, would you?"

"Well, you know . . . no. Not as such, but . . ."

"Not as such? Not die as such? But?" Trillian cocked her head on one side.

"Well, maybe someone else might have picked them up later."

"A second later and they would have been dead."

"Yeah, so if you'd taken the trouble to think about the problem a bit longer it would have gone away."

"You'd have been happy to let them die?"

"Well, you know, not happy as such, but . . ."

"Anyway," said Trillian, turning back to the controls, "I didn't pick them up."

"What do you mean? Who picked them up then?"

"The ship did."

"Huh?"

"The ship did. All by itself."

"Huh?"

"While we were in Improbability Drive."

"But that's incredible."

"No, Zaphod. Just very very improbable."

"Er, yeah."

"Look, Zaphod," she said, patting his arm, "don't worry

about the aliens. They're just a couple of guys, I expect. I'll send the robot down to get them and bring them up here. Hey, Marvin!"

In the corner, the robot's head swung up sharply, but then wobbled about imperceptibly. It pulled itself up to its feet as if it was about five pounds heavier than it actually was, and made what an outside observer would have thought was a heroic effort to cross the room. It stopped in front of Trillian and seemed to stare through her left shoulder.

"I think you ought to know I'm feeling very depressed," it said. Its voice was low and hopeless.

"Oh God," muttered Zaphod, and slumped into a seat.

"Well," said Trillian in a bright compassionate tone, "here's something to occupy you and keep your mind off things."

"It won't work," droned Marvin, "I have an exceptionally large mind."

"Marvin!" warned Trillian.

"All right," said Marvin, "what do you want me to do?"

"Go down to number two entry bay and bring the two aliens up here under surveillance."

With a microsecond pause, and a finely calculated micro-modulation of pitch and timbre—nothing you could actually take offense at—Marvin managed to convey his utter contempt and horror of all things human.

"Just that?" he said.

"Yes," said Trillian firmly.

"I won't enjoy it," said Marvin.

Zaphod leaped out of his seat.

"She's not asking you to enjoy it," he shouted, "just do it, will you?"

"All right," said Marvin, like the tolling of a great cracked bell, "I'll do it."

"Good . . ." snapped Zaphod, "great . . . thank you . . ."

Marvin turned and lifted his flat-topped triangular red eyes up toward him.

"I'm not getting you down at all, am I?" he said pathetically.

"No no, Marvin," lilted Trillian, "that's just fine, really. . . ."

"I wouldn't like to think I was getting you down."

"No, don't worry about that," the lilt continued, "you just act as comes naturally and everything will be just fine."

"You're sure you don't mind?" probed Marvin.

"No, no, Marvin," lilted Trillian, "that's just fine, really . . . just part of life."

Marvin flashed her an electronic look.

"Life," said Marvin, "don't talk to me about life."

He turned hopelessly on his heel and lugged himself out of the cabin. With a satisfied hum and a click the door closed behind him.

"I don't think I can stand that robot much longer, Zaphod," growled Trillian.

The Encyclopedia Galactica *defines a robot as a mechanical apparatus designed to do the work of a man. The marketing division of the Sirius Cybernetics Corporation defines a robot as* "Your Plastic Pal Who's Fun to Be With."

The Hitchhiker's Guide to the Galaxy *defines the market-*

ing division of the Sirius Cybernetics Corporation as "a bunch of mindless jerks who'll be the first against the wall when the revolution comes," with a footnote to the effect that the editors would welcome applications from anyone interested in taking over the post of robotics correspondent.

Curiously enough, an edition of the Encyclopedia Galactica *that had the good fortune to fall through a time warp from a thousand years in the future defined the marketing division of the Sirius Cybernetics Corporation as "a bunch of mindless jerks who were the first against the wall when the revolution came."*

The pink cubicle had winked out of existence, the monkeys had sunk away to a better dimension. Ford and Arthur found themselves in the embarkation area of the ship. It was rather smart.

"I think this ship's brand new," said Ford.

"How can you tell?" asked Arthur. "Have you got some exotic device for measuring the age of metal?"

"No, I just found this sales brochure lying on the floor. It's a lot of 'the Universe can be yours' stuff. Ah! Look, I was right."

Ford jabbed at one of the pages and showed it to Arthur.

"It says: *'Sensational new breakthrough in Improbability Physics. As soon as the ship's drive reaches Infinite Improbability it passes through every point in the Universe. Be the envy of other major governments.'* Wow, this is big league stuff."

Ford hunted excitedly through the technical specs of the ship, occasionally gasping with astonishment at what he read—clearly Galactic astrotechnology had moved ahead during the years of his exile.

Arthur listened for a short while, but being unable to understand the vast majority of what Ford was saying, he began to let his mind wander, trailing his fingers along the edge of an incomprehensible computer bank. He reached out and pressed an invitingly large red button on a nearby panel. The panel lit up with the words *Please do not press this button again.* He shook himself.

"Listen," said Ford, who was still engrossed in the sales brochure, "they make a big thing of the ship's cybernetics. *'A new generation of Sirius Cybernetics Corporation robots and computers, with the new GPP feature.'"*

"GPP feature?" said Arthur. "What's that?"

"Oh, it says *Genuine People Personalities.*"

"Oh," said Arthur, "sounds ghastly."

A voice behind them said, "It is." The voice was low and hopeless and accompanied by a slight clanking sound. They spun round and saw an abject steel man standing hunched in the doorway.

"What?" they said.

"Ghastly," continued Marvin, "it all is. Absolutely ghastly. Just don't even talk about it. Look at this door," he said, stepping through it. The irony circuits cut in to his voice modulator as he mimicked the style of the sales brochure. "*'All the doors in this spaceship have a cheerful and sunny disposition. It is their pleasure to open for you, and their satisfaction to close again with the knowledge of a job well done.'"*

As the door closed behind them it became apparent that

it did indeed have a satisfied sighlike quality to it. *"Humm-mmmmmyummmmmmmm ah!"* it said.

Marvin regarded it with cold loathing while his logic circuits chattered with disgust and tinkered with the concept of directing physical violence against it. Further circuits cut in saying, *Why bother? What's the point? Nothing is worth getting involved in.* Further circuits amused themselves by analyzing the molecular components of the door, and of the humanoids' brain cells. For a quick encore they measured the level of hydrogen emissions in the surrounding cubic parsec of space and then shut down again in boredom. A spasm of despair shook the robot's body as he turned.

"Come on," he droned, "I've been ordered to take you down to the bridge. Here I am, brain the size of a planet and they ask me to take you down to the bridge. Call that *job satisfaction?* 'Cos I don't."

He turned and walked back to the hated door.

"Er, excuse me," said Ford following after him, "which government owns this ship?"

Marvin ignored him.

"You watch this door," he muttered, "it's about to open again. I can tell by the intolerable air of smugness it suddenly generates."

With an ingratiating little whine the door slid open again and Marvin stomped through.

"Come on," he said.

The others followed quickly and the door slid back into place with pleased little clicks and whirrs.

"Thank you the marketing division of the Sirius Cybernetics Corporation," said Marvin, and trudged desolately up the gleaming curved corridor that stretched out before them. *"Let's build robots with Genuine People Personalities,"* they said. So they tried it out with me. I'm a personality prototype. You can tell, can't you?"

Ford and Arthur muttered embarrassed little disclaimers.

"I hate that door," continued Marvin. "I'm not getting you down at all, am I?"

"Which government . . ." started Ford again.

"No government owns it," snapped the robot, "it's been stolen."

"Stolen?"

"Stolen?" mimicked Marvin.

"Who by?" asked Ford.

"Zaphod Beeblebrox."

Something extraordinary happened to Ford's face. At least five entirely separate and distinct expressions of shock and amazement piled up on it in a jumbled mess. His left leg, which was in midstride, seemed to have difficulty in finding the floor again. He stared at the robot and tried to disentangle some dartoid muscles.

"Zaphod Beeblebrox . . .?" he said weakly.

"Sorry, did I say something wrong?" said Marvin, dragging himself on regardless. "Pardon me for breathing, which I never do anyway so I don't know why I bother to say it, oh God, I'm so depressed. Here's another of those self-satisfied doors. *Life!* Don't talk to me about life."

"No one even mentioned it," muttered Arthur irritably. "Ford, are you all right?"

Ford stared at him. "Did that robot say Zaphod Beeblebrox?" he said.

Chapter 12

A loud clatter of gunk music flooded through the Heart of Gold cabin as Zaphod searched the sub-etha radio wave bands for news of himself. The machine was rather difficult to operate. For years radios had been operated by means of pressing buttons and turning dials; then as the technology became more sophisticated the controls were made touch-sensitive—you merely had to brush the panels with your fingers; now all you had to do was wave your hand in the general direction of the components and hope. It saved a lot of muscular expenditure, of course, but meant that you had to sit infuriatingly still if you wanted to keep listening to the same program.

Zaphod waved a hand and the channel switched again. More gunk music, but this time it was a background to a news announcement. The news was always heavily edited to fit the rhythms of the music.

"... *and news reports brought to you here on the sub-etha wave band, broadcasting around the Galaxy around the clock,*" squawked a voice, "*and we'll be saying a big hello to all intelligent life forms everywhere ... and to everyone else out there, the secret is to bang the rocks together, guys. And of course, the big news story tonight is the sensational theft of the new Improbability Drive prototype ship by none other than Galactic President Zaphod Beeblebrox. And the question everyone's asking is . . . has the Big Z finally flipped? Beeblebrox, the man who invented the Pan Galactic Gargle Blaster, exconfidence trickster, once described by Eccentrica Gallumbits as the Best Bang since the Big One, and recently voted the Worst Dressed Sentient Being in the Known Universe for the seventh time . . . has he got an answer this time? We asked his private brain care specialist Gag Halfrunt . . ."*

The music swirled and dived for a moment. Another voice broke in, presumably Halfrunt. He said *"Vell, Zaphod's just zis guy, you know?"* but got no further because an electric pencil flew across the cabin and through the radio's on/off-sensitive airspace. Zaphod turned and glared at Trillian—she had thrown the pencil.

"Hey," he said, "what you do that for?"

Trillian was tapping her finger on a screenful of figures.

"I've just thought of something," she said.

"Yeah? Worth interrupting a news bulletin about me for?"

"You hear enough about yourself as it is."

"I'm very insecure. We know that."

"Can we drop your ego for a moment? This is important."

"If there's anything more important than my ego around, I want it caught and shot now." Zaphod glared at her again, then laughed.

"Listen," she said, "we picked up those couple of guys . . ."

"What couple of guys?"

"The couple of guys we picked up."

"Oh yeah," said Zaphod, "those couple of guys."

"We picked them up in sector ZZ$_9$ Plural Z Alpha."

"Yeah?" said Zaphod, and blinked.

Trillian said quietly, "Does that mean anything to you?"

"Mmmm," said Zaphod, "ZZ$_9$ Plural Z Alpha. ZZ$_9$ Plural Z Alpha?"

"Well?" said Trillian.

"Er . . . what does the Z mean?" said Zaphod.

"Which one?"

"Any one."

One of the major difficulties Trillian experienced in her relationship with Zaphod was learning to distinguish between him pretending to be stupid just to get people off their guard, pretending to be stupid because he couldn't be bothered to think and wanted someone else to do it for him, pretending to be outrageously stupid to hide the fact that he actually didn't understand what was going on, and really being genuinely stupid. He was renowned for being amazingly clever and quite clearly was so—but not all the time, which obviously worried him, hence the act. He preferred people to be puzzled rather than contemptuous. This above all appeared to Trillian to be genuinely stupid, but she could no longer be bothered to argue about it.

She sighed and punched up a star map on the visiscreen so she could make it simple for him, whatever his reasons for wanting it to be that way.

"There," she pointed, "right there."

"Hey . . . yeah!" said Zaphod.

"Well?" she said.

"Well what?"

Parts of the inside of her head screamed at other parts of the inside of her head. She said, very calmly, "It's the same sector you originally picked me up in."

He looked at her and then looked back at the screen.

"Hey, yeah," he said, "now that is wild. We should have zapped straight into the middle of the Horsehead Nebula. How did we come to be there? I mean, that's nowhere."

She ignored this.

"Improbability Drive," she said patiently. "You explained it to me yourself. We pass through every point in the Universe, you know that."

"Yeah, but that's one wild coincidence, isn't it?"

"Yes."

"Picking someone up at that point? Out of the whole of the Universe to choose from? That's just too . . . I want to work this out. Computer!"

The Sirius Cybernetics Shipboard Computer, which controlled and permeated every particle of the ship, switched into communication mode.

"Hi there!" it said brightly and simultaneously spewed out a tiny ribbon of ticker tape just for the record. The ticker tape said, *Hi there!*

"Oh God," said Zaphod. He hadn't worked with this computer for long but had already learned to loathe it.

The computer continued, brash and cheery as if it were selling detergent.

"I want you to know that whatever your problem, I am here to help you solve it."

"Yeah, yeah," said Zaphod. "Look, I think I'll just use a piece of paper."

"Sure thing," said the computer, spilling out its message into a waste bin at the same time, "I understand. If you ever want . . ."

"Shut up!" said Zaphod, and snatching up a pencil sat down next to Trillian at the console.

"Okay, okay," said the computer in a hurt tone of voice and closed down its speech channel again.

Zaphod and Trillian pored over the figures that the Improbability flight-path scanner flashed silently up in front of them.

"Can we work out," said Zaphod, "from their point of view what the Improbability of their rescue was?"

"Yes, that's a constant," said Trillian, "two to the power of two hundred and seventy-six thousand, seven hundred and nine to one against."

"That's high. They're two lucky lucky guys."

"Yes."

"But relative to what we were doing when the ship picked them up . . ."

Trillian punched up the figures. They showed two-to-the-power-of-Infinity-minus-one to one against (an irrational number that only has a conventional meaning in Improbability Physics).

"It's pretty low," continued Zaphod with a slight whistle.

"Yes," agreed Trillian, and looked at him quizzically.

"That's one big whack of Improbability to be accounted for. Something pretty improbable has got to show up on the balance sheet if it's all going to add up into a pretty sum."

Zaphod scribbled a few sums, crossed them out and threw the pencil away.

"Bat's dos, I can't work it out."

"Well?"

Zaphod knocked his two heads together in irritation and gritted his teeth.

"Okay," he said. "Computer!"

The voice circuits sprang to life again.

"Why, hello there!" they said (ticker tape, ticker tape). "All I want to do is make your day nicer and nicer and nicer. . ."

"Yeah, well, shut up and work something out for me."

"Sure thing," chattered the computer, "you want a probability forecast based on . . ."

"Improbability data, yeah."

"Okay," the computer continued. "Here's an interesting little notion. Did you realize that most people's lives are governed by telephone numbers?"

A pained look crawled across one of Zaphod's faces and on to the other one.

"Have you flipped?" he said.

"No, but you will when I tell you that . . ."

Trillian gasped. She scrabbled at the buttons on the Improbability flight-path screen.

"Telephone number?" she said. "Did that thing say *telephone number?*"

Numbers flashed up on the screen.

The computer had paused politely, but now it continued. "What I was about to say was that . . ."

"Don't bother, please," said Trillian.

"Look, what is this?" said Zaphod.

"I don't know," said Trillian, "but those aliens—they're on the way up to the bridge with that wretched robot. Can we pick them up on any monitor cameras?"

Chapter 13

Marvin trudged on down the corridor, still moaning.

"And then of course I've got this terrible pain in all the diodes down my left-hand side . . ."

"No?" said Arthur grimly as he walked along beside him. "Really?"

"Oh yes," said Marvin, "I mean I've asked for them to be replaced but no one ever listens."

"I can imagine."

Vague whistling and humming noises were coming from Ford. "Well well well," he kept saying to himself, "Zaphod Beeblebrox . . ."

Suddenly Marvin stopped, and held up a hand.

"You know what's happened now, of course?"

"No, what?" said Arthur, who didn't want to know.

"We've arrived at another of those doors."

There was a sliding door let into the side of the corridor. Marvin eyed it suspiciously.

"Well?" said Ford impatiently. "Do we go through?"

"*Do we go through?*" mimicked Marvin. "Yes. This is the entrance to the bridge. I was told to take you to the bridge. Probably the highest demand that will be made on my intellectual capacities today, I shouldn't wonder."

Slowly, with great loathing, he stepped toward the door, like a hunter stalking his prey. Suddenly it slid open.

"*Thank you,*" it said, "*for making a simple door very happy.*"

Deep in Marvin's thorax gears ground.

"Funny," he intoned funereally, "how just when you think life can't possibly get any worse it suddenly does."

He heaved himself through the door and left Ford and Arthur staring at each other and shrugging their shoulders. From inside they heard Marvin's voice again.

"I suppose you'll want to see the aliens now," he said. "Do you want me to sit in a corner and rust, or just fall apart where I'm standing?"

"Yeah, just show them in, would you, Marvin?" came another voice.

Arthur looked at Ford and was astonished to see him laughing.

"What's . . .?"

"Shhh," said Ford, "come on in."

He stepped through into the bridge.

Arthur followed him in nervously and was astonished to see a man lolling back in a chair with his feet on a control console picking the teeth in his right-hand head with his left hand. The right-hand head seemed to be thoroughly preoccupied with this task, but the left-hand one was grinning a broad, relaxed, nonchalant grin. The number of things that Arthur couldn't believe he was seeing was fairly large. His jaw flopped about at a loose end for a while.

. The peculiar man waved a lazy wave at Ford and with an

appalling affectation of nonchalance said, "Ford, hi, how are you? Glad you could drop in."

Ford was not going to be outcooled.

"Zaphod," he drawled, "great to see you, you're looking well, the extra arm suits you. Nice ship you've stolen."

Arthur goggled at him.

"You mean you know this guy?" he said, waving a wild finger at Zaphod.

"Know him!" exclaimed Ford, "he's . . ." he paused, and decided to do the introductions the other way round.

"Oh, Zaphod, this is a friend of mine, Arthur Dent," he said, "I saved him when his planet blew up."

"Oh sure," said Zaphod, "hi, Arthur, glad you could make it." His right-hand head looked round casually, said "hi" and went back to having its teeth picked.

Ford carried on. "And Arthur," he said, "this is my semicousin Zaphod Beeb . . ."

"We've met," said Arthur sharply.

When you're cruising down the road in the fast lane and you lazily sail past a few hard-driving cars and are feeling pretty pleased with yourself and then accidentally change down from fourth to first instead of third thus making your engine leap out of your hood in a rather ugly mess, it tends to throw you off your stride in much the same way that this remark threw Ford Prefect off his.

"Er . . . what?" he said.

"I said we've met."

Zaphod gave an awkward start of surprise and jabbed a gum sharply.

"Hey . . . er, have we? Hey . . . er . . ."

Ford rounded on Arthur with an angry flash in his eyes. Now he felt he was back on home ground he suddenly began to resent having lumbered himself with this ignorant primitive who knew as much about the affairs of the Galaxy as an Ilford-based gnat knew about life in Peking.

"What do you mean you've met?" he demanded. "This is Zaphod Beeblebrox from Betelgeuse Five, you know, not bloody Martin Smith from Croydon."

"I don't care," said Arthur coldly. "We've met, haven't we, Zaphod Beeblebrox—or should I say . . . Phil?"

"What!" shouted Ford.

"You'll have to remind me," said Zaphod. "I've a terrible memory for species."

"It was at a party," pursued Arthur.

"Yeah, well, I doubt that," said Zaphod.

"Cool it, will you, Arthur!" demanded Ford.

Arthur would not be deterred. "A party six months ago. On Earth . . . England . . ."

Zaphod shook his head with a tight-lipped smile.

"London," insisted Arthur, "Islington."

"Oh," said Zaphod with a guilty start, "*that* party."

This wasn't fair on Ford at all. He looked backward and forward between Arthur and Zaphod. "What?" he said to Zaphod. "You don't mean to say you've been on that miserable little planet as well, do you?"

"No, of course not," said Zaphod breezily. "Well, I may have just dropped in briefly, you know, on my way somewhere. . ."

"But I was stuck there for fifteen years!"

"Well, I didn't know that, did I?"

"But what were you doing there?"

"Looking about, you know."

"He gate-crashed a party," said Arthur, trembling with anger, "a fancy dress party . . ."

"It would have to be, wouldn't it?" said Ford.

"At this party," persisted Arthur, "was a girl . . . oh, well, look, it doesn't matter now. The whole place has gone up in smoke anyway . . ."

"I wish you'd stop sulking about that bloody planet," said Ford. "Who was the lady?"

"Oh, just somebody. Well all right, I wasn't doing very well with her. I'd been trying all evening. Hell, she was something though. Beautiful, charming, devastatingly intelligent, at last I'd got her to myself for a bit and was plying her with a bit of talk when this friend of yours barges up and says 'Hey, doll, is this guy boring you? Why don't you talk to me instead? I'm from a different planet.' I never saw her again."

"Zaphod?" exclaimed Ford.

"Yes," said Arthur, glaring at him and trying not to feel foolish. "He only had the two arms and the one head and he called himself Phil, but . . ."

"But you must admit he did turn out to be from another planet," said Trillian, wandering into sight at the other end of the bridge. She gave Arthur a pleasant smile which settled on him like a ton of bricks and then turned her attention to the ship's controls again.

There was silence for a few seconds, and then out of the scrambled mess of Arthur's brain crawled some words.

"Tricia McMillan?" he said. "What are you doing here?"

"Same as you," she said, "I hitched a lift. After all, with a degree in math and another in astrophysics what else was there to do? It was either that or the dole queue again on Monday."

"Infinity minus one," chattered the computer. "Improbability sum now complete."

Zaphod looked about him, at Ford, at Arthur, and then at Trillian.

"Trillian," he said, "is this sort of thing going to happen every time we use the Improbability Drive?"

"Very probably, I'm afraid," she said.

Chapter 14

The Heart of Gold fled on silently through the night of space, now on conventional photon drive. Its crew of four were ill at ease knowing that they had been brought together not of their own volition or by simple coincidence, but by some curious perversion of physics—as if relationships between people were susceptible to the same laws that governed the relationships between atoms and molecules.

As the ship's artificial night closed in they were each grateful to retire to separate cabins and try to rationalize their thoughts.

Trillian couldn't sleep. She sat on a couch and stared at a small cage which contained her last and only links with Earth—two white mice that she had insisted Zaphod let her bring. She had expected never to see the planet again, but she was disturbed by her negative reaction to the news of the planet's destruction. It seemed remote and unreal and she could find no thoughts to think about it. She watched the mice scurrying round the cage and running furiously in their little plastic treadwheels till they occupied her whole attention. Suddenly she shook herself and went back on to the bridge to watch over the tiny flashing lights and figures that charted the ship's progress through the void. She wished she knew what it was she was trying not to think about.

Zaphod couldn't sleep. He also wished he knew what it was that he wouldn't let himself think about. For as long as he could remember he'd suffered from a vague nagging feeling of being not all there. Most of the time he was able to put this thought aside and not worry about it, but it had been reawakened by the sudden, inexplicable arrival of Ford Prefect and Arthur Dent. Somehow it seemed to conform to a pattern that he couldn't see.

Ford couldn't sleep. He was too excited about being back on the road again. Fifteen years of virtual imprisonment were over, just as he was finally beginning to give up hope. Knocking about with Zaphod for a bit promised to be a lot of fun, though there seemed to be something faintly odd about his semicousin that he couldn't put his finger on. The fact that he had become President of the Galaxy was frankly astonishing, as was the manner of his leaving the post. Was there a reason behind it? There would be no point in asking Zaphod, he never appeared to have a reason for anything he did at all: he had turned unfathomability into an art form. He attacked everything in life with a mixture of extraordinary genius and naive incompetence and it was often difficult to tell which was which.

Arthur slept: he was terribly tired.

There was a tap at Zaphod's door. It slid open.

"Zaphod . . . ?"

"Yeah?"

Trillian stood outlined in the oval of light.

"I think we just found what you came to look for."

"Hey, yeah?"

Ford gave up the attempt to sleep. In the corner of his cabin was a small computer screen and keyboard. He sat at it for a while and tried to compose a new entry for the *Guide* on the subject of Vogons but couldn't think of anything vitriolic enough so he gave that up too, wrapped a robe round himself and went for a walk to the bridge.

As he entered he was surprised to see two figures hunched excitedly over the instruments.

"See? The ship's about to move into orbit," Trillian was saying. "There's a planet out there. It's at the exact coordinates you predicted."

Zaphod heard a noise and looked up.

"Ford!" he hissed. "Hey, come and take a look at this."

Ford went and had a look at it. It was a series of figures flickering over a screen.

"You recognize those Galactic coordinates?" said Zaphod.

"No."

"I'll give you a clue. Computer!"

"Hi, gang!" enthused the computer. "This is getting real sociable, isn't it?"

"Shut up," said Zaphod, "and show up the screens."

Light on the bridge sank. Pinpoints of light played across the consoles and reflected in four pairs of eyes that stared up at the external monitor screens.

There was absolutely nothing on them.

"Recognize that?" whispered Zaphod.

Ford frowned.

"Er, no," he said.

"What do you see?"

"Nothing."

"Recognize it?"

"What are you talking about?"

"We're in the Horsehead Nebula. One whole vast dark cloud."

"And I was meant to recognize that from a blank screen?"

"Inside a dark nebula is the only place in the Galaxy you'd see a dark screen."

"Very good."

Zaphod laughed. He was clearly very excited about something, almost childishly so.

"Hey, this is really terrific, this is just far too much!"

"What's so great about being stuck in a dust cloud?" said Ford.

"What would you reckon to find here?" urged Zaphod.

"Nothing."

"No stars? No planets?"

"No."

"Computer!" shouted Zaphod, "rotate angle of vision through one-eighty degrees and don't talk about it!"

For a moment it seemed that nothing was happening, then a brightness glowed at the edge of the huge screen. A red star the size of a small plate crept across it followed quickly by another one—a binary system. Then a vast crescent sliced into the corner of the picture—a red glare shading away into deep black, the night side of the planet.

"I've found it!" cried Zaphod, thumping the console. "I've found it!"

Ford stared at it in astonishment.

"What is it?" he said.

"That . . ." said Zaphod, "is the most improbable planet that ever existed."

Chapter 15

(Excerpt from *The Hitchhiker's Guide to the Galaxy*, page 634784, section 5a. Entry: *Magrathea*)

Far back in the mists of ancient time, in the great and glorious days of the former Galactic Empire, life was wild, rich and largely tax free.

Mighty starships plied their way between exotic suns, seeking adventure and reward among the furthest reaches of Galactic space. In those days spirits were brave, the stakes were high, men were real men, women were real women and small furry creatures from Alpha Centauri were real small furry creatures from Alpha Centauri. And all dared to brave unknown terrors, to do mighty deeds, to boldly split infinitives that no man had split before—and thus was the Empire forged.

Many men of course became extremely rich, but this was perfectly natural and nothing to be ashamed of because no one was really poor—at least no one worth speaking of. And for all the richest and most successful merchants life inevitably became rather dull and niggly, and they began to imagine that this was therefore the fault of the worlds they'd settled on. None of them was entirely satisfactory: either the climate wasn't quite right in the later part of the afternoon, or the day was half an hour too long, or the sea was exactly the wrong shade of pink.

And thus were created the conditions for a staggering new

form of specialist industry: custom-made luxury planet build-ing. The home of this industry was the planet Magrathea, where hyperspatial engineers sucked matter through white holes in space to form it into dream planets—gold planets, plat-imum planets, soft rubber planets with lots of earthquakes—all lovingly made to meet the exacting standards that the Galaxy's richest men naturally came to expect.

But so successful was this venture that Magrathea itself soon became the richest planet of all time and the rest of the Galaxy was reduced to abject poverty. And so the system broke down, the Empire collapsed, and a long sullen silence settled over a billion hungry worlds, disturbed only by the pen scratchings of scholars as they labored into the night over smug little treatises on the value of a planned political economy.

Magrathea itself disappeared and its memory soon passed into the obscurity of legend.

In these enlightened days, of course, no one believes a word of it.

Chapter 16

Arthur awoke to the sound of argument and went to the bridge. Ford was waving his arms about.

"You're crazy, Zaphod," he was saying, "Magrathea is a myth, a fairy story, it's what parents tell their kids about at night if they want them to grow up to become economists, it's . . ."

"And that's what we are currently in orbit about," insisted Zaphod.

"Look, I can't help what you may personally be in orbit around," said Ford, "but this ship . . ."

"Computer!" shouted Zaphod.

"Oh no . . ."

"Hi there! This is Eddie, your shipboard computer, and I'm feeling just great, guys, and I know I'm just going to get a bundle of kicks out of any program you care to run through me."

Arthur looked inquiringly at Trillian. She motioned him to come on in but keep quiet.

"Computer," said Zaphod, "tell us what our present trajectory is."

"A real pleasure, feller," it burbled; "we are currently in orbit at an altitude of three hundred miles around the legendary planet of Magrathea."

"Proving nothing," said Ford. "I wouldn't trust that computer to speak my weight."

"I can do that for you, sure," enthused the computer, punching out more ticker tape. "I can even work out your personality problems to ten decimal places if it will help."

Trillian interrupted.

"Zaphod," she said, "any minute now we will be swinging round to the daylight side of this planet," adding, "whatever it turns out to be."

"Hey, what do you mean by that? The planet's where I predicted it would be, isn't it?"

"Yes, I know there's a planet there. I'm not arguing with anyone, it's just that I wouldn't know Magrathea from any other lump of cold rock. Dawn's coming up if you want it."

"Okay, okay," muttered Zaphod, "let's at least give our eyes a good time. Computer!"

"Hi there! What can I . . ."

"Just shut up and give us a view of the planet again."

A dark featureless mass once more filled the screens—the planet rolling away beneath them.

They watched for a moment in silence, but Zaphod was fidgety with excitement.

"We are now traversing the night side . . ." he said in a hushed voice. The planet rolled on.

"The surface of the planet is now three hundred miles beneath us . . ." he continued. He was trying to restore a sense of occasion to what he felt should have been a great moment. Magrathea! He was piqued by Ford's skeptical reaction. Magrathea!

"In a few seconds," he continued, "we should see . . . there!"

The moment carried itself. Even the most seasoned star tramp can't help but shiver at the spectacular drama of a sunrise seen from space, but a binary sunrise is one of the marvels of the Galaxy.

Out of the utter blackness stabbed a sudden point of blinding light. It crept up by slight degrees and spread sideways in a thin crescent blade, and within seconds two suns were visible, furnaces of light, searing the black edge of the horizon with white fire. Fierce shafts of color streaked through the thin atmosphere beneath them.

"The fires of dawn . . . !" breathed Zaphod. "The twin suns of Soulianis and Rahm . . . !"

"Or whatever," said Ford quietly.

"Soulianis and Rahm!" insisted Zaphod.

The suns blazed into the pitch of space and a low ghostly music floated through the bridge: Marvin was humming ironically because he hated humans so much.

As Ford gazed at the spectacle of light before them excitement burned inside him, but only the excitement of seeing a strange new planet; it was enough for him to see it as it was. It faintly irritated him that Zaphod had to impose some ludicrous fantasy onto the scene to make it work for him. All this Magrathea nonsense seemed juvenile. Isn't it enough to see that a garden is beautiful without having to believe that there are fairies at the bottom of it too?

All this Magrathea business seemed totally incomprehensible to Arthur. He edged up to Trillian and asked her what was going on.

"I only know what Zaphod's told me," she whispered. "Apparently Magrathea is some kind of legend from way back which no one seriously believes in. Bit like Atlantis on Earth, except that the legends say the Magratheans used to manufacture planets."

Arthur blinked at the screens and felt he was missing something important. Suddenly he realized what it was.

"Is there any tea on this spaceship?" he asked.

More of the planet was unfolding beneath them as the Heart of Gold streaked along its orbital path. The suns now stood high in the black sky, the pyrotechnics of dawn were over, and the surface of the planet appeared bleak and forbidding in the common light of day—gray, dusty and only dimly contoured. It looked dead and cold as a crypt. From time to time promising features would appear on the distant horizon—ravines, maybe mountains, maybe even cities—but as they approached the lines would soften and blur into anonymity and nothing would transpire. The planet's surface was blurred by time, by the slow movement of the thin stagnant air that had crept across it for century upon century.

Clearly, it was very very old.

A moment of doubt came to Ford as he watched the gray landscape move beneath them. The immensity of time worried him, he could feel it as a presence. He cleared his throat.

"Well, even supposing it is . . ."

"It is," said Zaphod.

"Which it isn't," continued Ford. "What do you want with it anyway? There's nothing there."

"Not on the surface," said Zaphod.

"All right, just supposing there's something, I take it you're not here for the sheer industrial archeology of it all. What are you after?"

One of Zaphod's heads looked away. The other one looked round to see what the first was looking at, but it wasn't looking at anything very much.

"Well," said Zaphod airily, "it's partly the curiosity, partly a sense of adventure, but mostly I think it's the fame and the money. . . ."

Ford glanced at him sharply. He got a very strong impression that Zaphod hadn't the faintest idea why he was there at all.

"You know, I don't like the look of that planet at all," said Trillian, shivering.

"Ah, take no notice," said Zaphod; "with half the wealth of the former Galactic Empire stored on it somewhere it can afford to look frumpy."

Bullshit, thought Ford. Even supposing this was the home of some ancient civilization now gone to dust, even supposing a number of exceedingly unlikely things, there was no way that vast treasures of wealth were going to be stored there in any form that would still have meaning now. He shrugged.

"I think it's just a dead planet," he said.

"The suspense is killing me," said Arthur testily.

Stress and nervous tension are now serious social problems in all parts of the Galaxy, and it is in order that this situation should not be in any way exacerbated that the following facts will now be revealed in advance.

The planet in question *is* in fact the legendary Magrathea.

The deadly missile attack shortly to be launched by an ancient automatic defense system will result merely in the breakage of three coffee cups and a mouse cage, the bruising of somebody's upper arm, and the untimely creation and sudden demise of a bowl of petunias and an innocent sperm whale.

In order that some sense of mystery should still be preserved, no revelation will yet be made concerning whose upper arm sustains the bruise. This fact may safely be made the subject of suspense since it is of no significance whatsoever.

Chapter 17

After a fairly shaky start to the day, Arthur's mind was beginning to reassemble itself from the shell-shocked fragments the previous day had left him with. He had found a Nutri-Matic machine which had provided him with a plastic cup filled with a liquid that was almost, but not quite, entirely unlike tea. The way it functioned was very interesting. When the *Drink* button was pressed it made an instant but highly detailed examination of the subject's taste buds, a spectroscopic analysis of the subject's metabolism and then sent tiny experimental signals down the neural pathways to the taste centers of the subject's brain to see what was likely to go down well. However, no one knew quite why it did this because it invariably delivered a cupful of liquid that was almost, but not quite, entirely unlike tea. The Nutri-Matic was designed and manufactured by the Sirius Cybernetics Corporation whose complaints department now covers all the major landmasses of the first three planets in the Sirius Tau Star system.

Arthur drank the liquid and found it reviving. He glanced up at the screens again and watched a few more hundred miles of barren grayness slide past. It suddenly occurred to him to ask a question that had been bothering him.

"Is it safe?" he said.

"Magrathea's been dead for five million years," said Zaphod; "of course it's safe. Even the ghosts will have settled down and raised families by now."

At which point a strange and inexplicable sound thrilled suddenly through the bridge—a noise as of a distant fanfare; a hollow, reedy, insubstantial sound. It preceded a voice that was equally hollow, reedy and insubstantial. The voice said, *"Greetings to you . . ."*

Someone from the dead planet was talking to them.

"Computer!" shouted Zaphod.

"Hi there!"

"What the photon is it?"

"Oh, just some five-million-year-old tape that's being broadcast at us."

"A what? A recording?"

"Shush!" said Ford. "It's carrying on."

The voice was old, courteous, almost charming, but was underscored with quite unmistakable menace.

"This is a recorded announcement," it said, *"as I'm afraid we're all out at the moment. The commercial council of Magrathea thanks you for your esteemed visit . . ."*

("A voice from ancient Magrathea!" shouted Zaphod. "Okay, okay," said Ford.)

". . . but regrets," continued the voice, *"that the entire planet is temporarily closed for business. Thank you. If you would care to leave your name and the address of a planet where you can be contacted, kindly speak when you hear the tone."*

A short buzz followed, then silence.

"They want to get rid of us," said Trillian nervously. "What do we do?"

"It's just a recording," said Zaphod. "We keep going. Got that, computer?"

"I got it," said the computer and gave the ship an extra kick of speed.

They waited.

After a second or so came the fanfare once again, and then the voice.

"We would like to assure you that as soon as our business is resumed announcements will be made in all fashionable magazines and color supplements, when our clients will once again be able to select from all that's best in contemporary geography." The menace in the voice took on a sharper edge. *"Meanwhile, we thank our clients for their kind interest and would ask them to leave. Now."*

Arthur looked round the nervous faces of his companions.

"Well, I suppose we'd better be going then, hadn't we?" he suggested.

"Shhh!" said Zaphod. "There's absolutely nothing to be worried about."

"Then why's everyone so tense?"

"They're just interested!" shouted Zaphod. "Computer, start a descent into the atmosphere and prepare for landing."

This time the fanfare was quite perfunctory, the voice now distinctly cold.

"It is most gratifying," it said, *"that your enthusiasm for our planet continues unabated, and so we would like to assure*

you that the guided missiles currently converging with your ship are part of a special service we extend to all of our most enthusiastic clients, and the fully armed nuclear warheads are of course merely a courtesy detail. We look forward to your custom in future lives. . . . Thank you."

The voice snapped off.

"Oh," said Trillian.

"Er . . ." said Arthur.

"Well?" said Ford.

"Look," said Zaphod, "will you get it into your heads? That's just a recorded message. It's millions of years old. It doesn't apply to us, get it?"

"What," said Trillian quietly, "about the missiles?"

"Missiles? Don't make me laugh."

Ford tapped Zaphod on the shoulder and pointed at the rear screen. Clear in the distance behind them two silver darts were climbing through the atmosphere toward the ship. A quick change of magnification brought them into close focus—two massively real rockets thundering through the sky. The suddenness of it was shocking.

"I think they're going to have a very good try at applying to us," said Ford.

Zaphod stared at them in astonishment.

"Hey, this is terrific!" he said. "Someone down there is trying to kill us!"

"Terrific," said Arthur.

"But don't you see what this means?"

"Yes. We're going to die."

"Yes, but apart from that."

"*Apart* from that?"

"It means we must be on to something!"

"How soon can we get off it?"

Second by second the image of the missiles on the screen grew larger. They had swung round now on to a direct homing course so that all that could be seen of them now was the warheads, head-on.

"As a matter of interest," said Trillian, "what are we going to do?"

"Just keep cool," said Zaphod.

"Is that all?" shouted Arthur.

"No, we're also going to . . . er . . . take evasive action!" said Zaphod with a sudden access of panic. "Computer, what evasive action can we take?"

"Er, none, I'm afraid, guys," said the computer.

"Or something," said Zaphod, ". . . er . . ." he said.

"There seems to be something jamming my guidance systems," explained the computer brightly, "impact minus forty-five seconds. Please call me Eddie if it will help you to relax."

Zaphod tried to run in several equally decisive directions simultaneously. "Right!" he said. "Er . . . we've got to get manual control of this ship."

"Can you fly her?" asked Ford pleasantly.

"No, can you?"

"No."

"Trillian, can you?"

"No."

"Fine," said Zaphod, relaxing. "We'll do it together."

"I can't either," said Arthur, who felt it was time he began to assert himself.

"I'd guessed that," said Zaphod. "Okay, computer, I want full manual control now."

"You got it," said the computer.

Several large desk panels slid open and banks of control consoles sprang up out of them, showering the crew with bits of expanded polystyrene packaging and balls of rolled-up cellophane: these controls had never been used before.

Zaphod stared at them wildly.

"Okay, Ford," he said, "full retro thrust and ten degrees starboard. Or something . . ."

"Good luck, guys," chirped the computer, "impact minus thirty seconds. . . ."

Ford leaped to the controls—only a few of them made any immediate sense to him so he pulled those. The ship shook and screamed as its guidance rocket jets tried to push it every which way simultaneously. He released half of them and the ship spun round in a tight arc and headed back the way it had come, straight toward the oncoming missiles.

Air cushions ballooned out of the walls in an instant as everyone was thrown against them. For a few seconds the inertial forces held them flattened and squirming for breath, unable to move. Zaphod struggled and pushed in manic desperation and finally managed a savage kick at a small lever that formed part of the guidance system.

The lever snapped off. The ship twisted sharply and rocketed upward. The crew were hurled violently back across the cabin. Ford's copy of *The Hitchhiker's Guide to the Galaxy* smashed into another section of the control console with the combined result that the *Guide* started to explain to anyone who cared to listen about the best ways of smuggling Antarean parakeet glands out of Antares (an Antarean parakeet gland stuck on a small stick is a revolting but much-sought-after cocktail delicacy and very large sums of money are often paid for them by very rich idiots who want to impress other very rich idiots), and the ship suddenly dropped out of the sky like a stone.

It was of course more or less at this moment that one of the crew sustained a nasty bruise to the upper arm. This should be emphasized because, as has already been revealed, they escape otherwise completely unharmed and the deadly nuclear missiles do not eventually hit the ship. The safety of the crew is absolutely assured.

"Impact minus twenty seconds, guys . . ." said the computer.

"Then turn the bloody engines back on!" bawled Zaphod.

"Oh, sure thing, guys," said the computer. With a subtle roar the engines cut back in, the ship smoothly flattened out of its dive and headed back toward the missiles again.

The computer started to sing.

"When you walk through the storm . . .'" it whined nasally, *" 'hold your head up high . . .'"*

Zaphod screamed at it to shut up, but his voice was lost in the din of what they quite naturally assumed was approaching destruction.

" 'And don't . . . be afraid . . . of the dark!' " Eddie wailed.

The ship, in flattening out, had in fact flattened out upside down and lying on the ceiling as they were it was now totally impossible for any of the crew to reach the guidance systems.

" '*At the end of the storm . . .*' " crooned Eddie.

The two missiles loomed massively on the screens as they thundered toward the ship.

" '*is a golden sky . . .*' "

But by an extraordinarily lucky chance they had not yet fully corrected their flight paths to that of the erratically weaving ship, and they passed right under it.

" '*And the sweet silver song of the lark.*' . . . Revised impact time fifteen seconds, fellas. . . . '*Walk on through the wind . . .*' "

The missiles banked round in a screeching arc and plunged back in pursuit.

"This is it," said Arthur watching them. "We are now quite definitely going to die, aren't we?"

"I wish you'd stop saying that," shouted Ford.

"Well, we are, aren't we?"

"Yes."

" '*Walk on through the rain . . .*' " sang Eddie.

A thought struck Arthur. He struggled to his feet.

"Why doesn't anyone turn on this Improbability Drive thing?" he said. "We could probably reach that."

"What are you, crazy?" said Zaphod. "Without proper programming anything could happen."

"Does that matter at this stage?" shouted Arthur.

" '*Though your dreams be tossed and blown . . .*' " sang Eddie.

Arthur scrambled up on to one of the excitingly chunky

pieces of molded contouring where the curve of the wall met the ceiling.

" '*Walk on, walk on, with hope in your heart . . .*' "

"Does anyone know why Arthur can't turn on the Improbability Drive?" shouted Trillian.

" '*And you'll never walk alone.*' . . . Impact minus five seconds, it's been great knowing you guys, God bless. . . . '*You'll ne . . . ver . . . walk . . . alone!*' "

"I said," yelled Trillian, "does anyone know . . ."

The next thing that happened was a mind-mangling explosion of noise and light.

nd the next thing that happened after that was that the Heart of Gold continued on its way perfectly normally with a rather fetchingly redesigned interior. It was somewhat larger, and done out in delicate pastel shades of green and blue. In the center a spiral staircase, leading nowhere in particular, stood in a spray of ferns and yellow flowers and next to it a stone sundial pedestal housed the main computer terminal. Cunningly deployed lighting and mirrors created the illusion of standing in a conservatory overlooking a wide stretch of exquisitely manicured garden. Around the periphery of the conservatory area stood marble-topped tables on intricately beautiful wrought-iron legs. As you gazed into the polished surface of the marble the vague forms of instruments became visible, and as you touched them the instruments materialized instantly under your hands. Looked at from the correct angles the mirrors appeared to reflect all the required data read-outs, though it was far from clear where they were reflected from. It was in fact sensationally beautiful.

Relaxing in a wickerwork sun chair, Zaphod Beeblebrox said, "What the hell happened?"

"Well, I was just saying," said Arthur lounging by a small fish pool, "there's this Improbability Drive switch over here . . ." he waved at where it had been. There was a potted plant there now.

"But where are we?" said Ford, who was sitting on the spiral staircase, a nicely chilled Pan Galactic Gargle Blaster in his hand.

"Exactly where we were, I think . . ." said Trillian, as all about them the mirrors suddenly showed them an image of the blighted landscape of Magrathea, which still scooted along beneath them.

Zaphod leaped out of his seat.

"Then what's happened to the missiles?" he said.

A new and astounding image appeared in the mirrors.

"They would appear," said Ford doubtfully, "to have turned into a bowl of petunias and a very surprised-looking whale . . ."

"At an Improbability factor," cut in Eddie, who hadn't changed a bit, "of eight million, seven hundred and sixty-seven thousand, one hundred and twenty-eight to one against."

Zaphod stared at Arthur.

"Did you think of that, Earthman?" he demanded.

"Well," said Arthur, "all I did was . . ."

"That's very good thinking, you know. Turn on the Improbability Drive for a second without first activating the proofing screens. Hey, kid, you just saved our lives, you know that?"

"Oh," said Arthur, "well, it was nothing really. . . ."

"Was it?" said Zaphod. "Oh well, forget it then. Okay, computer, take us in to land."

"But . . ."

"I said forget it."

Another thing that got forgotten was the fact that against all probability a sperm whale had suddenly been called into existence several miles above the surface of an alien planet.

And since this is not a naturally tenable position for a whale, this poor innocent creature had very little time to come to terms with its identity as a whale before it then had to come to terms with not being a whale any more.

This is a complete record of its thought from the moment it began its life till the moment it ended it.

Ah . . . ! What's happening? it thought.

Er, excuse me, who am I?

Hello?

Why am I here? What's my purpose in life?

What do I mean by who am I?

Calm down, get a grip now . . . oh! this is an interesting sensation, what is it? It's a sort of . . . yawning, tingling sensation in my . . . my . . . well, I suppose I'd better start finding names for things if I want to make any headway in what for the sake of what I shall call an argument I shall call the world, so let's call it my stomach.

Good. Ooooh, it's getting quite strong. And hey, what about this whistling roaring sound going past what I'm suddenly going to call my head? Perhaps I can call that . . . wind! Is that a good name? It'll do . . . perhaps I can find a better name for it later when I've found out what it's for. It must be something very important because there certainly seems to be a hell of a lot of it. Hey! What's this thing? This . . . let's call it a tail—yeah, tail. Hey! I can really thrash it about pretty good, can't I? Wow! Wow! That feels great! Doesn't seem to achieve very much but I'll probably find out what it's for later on. Now, have I built up any coherent picture of things yet?

No.

Never mind, hey, this is really exciting, so much to find out about, so much to look forward to, I'm quite dizzy with anticipation . . .

Or is it the wind?

There really is a lot of that now, isn't there?

And wow! Hey! What's this thing suddenly coming toward me very fast? Very, very fast. So big and flat and round, it needs a big wide-sounding name like . . . ow . . . ound . . . round . . . ground! That's it! That's a good name— ground!

I wonder if it will be friends with me?

And the rest, after a sudden wet thud, was silence.

Curiously enough, the only thing that went through the mind of the bowl of petunias as it fell was Oh no, not again. Many people have speculated that if we knew exactly why the bowl of petunias had thought that we would know a lot more about the nature of the Universe than we do now.

Chapter 19

Are we taking this robot with us?" said Ford, looking with distaste at Marvin, who was standing in an awkward hunched posture in the corner under a small palm tree.

Zaphod glanced away from the mirror screens which presented a panoramic view of the blighted landscape on which the Heart of Gold had now landed.

"Oh, the Paranoid Android," he said. "Yeah, we'll take him."

"But what are you supposed to do with a manically depressed robot?"

"You think you've got problems," said Marvin, as if he was addressing a newly occupied coffin, "what are you supposed to do if you *are* a manically depressed robot? No, don't bother to answer that, I'm fifty thousand times more intelligent than you and even I don't know the answer. It gives me a headache just trying to think down to your level."

Trillian burst in through the door from her cabin.

"My white mice have escaped!" she said.

An expression of deep worry and concern failed to cross either of Zaphod's faces.

"Nuts to your white mice," he said.

Trillian glared an upset glare at him, and disappeared again.

It is possible that her remark would have commanded greater attention had it been generally realized that human beings were only the third most intelligent life form present on the planet Earth, instead of (as was generally thought by most independent observers) the second.

"Good afternoon, boys."

The voice was oddly familiar, but oddly different. It had a matriarchal twang. It announced itself to the crew as they arrived at the airlock hatchway that would let them out on the planet surface.

They looked at each other in puzzlement.

"It's the computer," explained Zaphod. "I discovered it had an emergency back-up personality that I thought might work out better."

"Now this is going to be your first day out on a strange new planet," continued Eddie's new voice, "so I want you all wrapped up snug and warm, and no playing with any naughty bug-eyed monsters."

Zaphod tapped impatiently on the hatch.

"I'm sorry," he said, "I think we might be better off with a slide rule."

"Right!" snapped the computer. "Who said that?"

"Will you open up the exit hatch, please, computer?" said Zaphod, trying not to get angry.

"Not until whoever said that owns up," urged the computer, stamping a few synapses closed.

"Oh God," muttered Ford, slumped against a bulkhead.

He started to count to ten. He was desperately worried that one day sentient life forms would forget how to do this. Only by counting could humans demonstrate their independence of computers.

"Come on," said Eddie sternly.

"Computer . . ." began Zaphod.

"I'm waiting," interrupted Eddie. "I can wait all day if necessary. . . ."

"Computer . . ." said Zaphod again, who had been trying to think of some subtle piece of reasoning to put the computer down with, and had decided not to bother competing with it on its own ground, "if you don't open that exit hatch this moment I shall zap straight off to your major data banks and reprogram you with a very large ax, got that?"

Eddie, shocked, paused and considered this.

Ford carried on counting quietly. This is about the most aggressive thing you can do to a computer, the equivalent of going up to a human being and saying *Blood . . . blood . . . blood . . . blood . . .*

Finally Eddie said quietly, "I can see this relationship is something we're all going to have to work at," and the hatchway opened.

An icy wind ripped into them, they hugged themselves warmly and stepped down the ramp on to the barren dust of Magrathea.

"It'll all end in tears, I know it," shouted Eddie after them, and closed the hatchway again.

A few minutes later he opened and closed the hatchway again in response to a command that caught him entirely by surprise.

Chapter 20

ive figures wandered slowly over the blighted land. Bits of it were dullish gray, bits of it dullish brown, the rest of it rather less interesting to look at. It was like a dried-out marsh, now barren of all vegetation and covered with a layer of dust about an inch thick. It was very cold.

Zaphod was clearly rather depressed about it. He stalked off by himself and was soon lost to sight behind a slight rise in the ground.

The wind stung Arthur's eyes and ears, and the stale thin air clasped his throat. However, the thing that was stung most was his mind.

"It's fantastic . . ." he said, and his own voice rattled his ears. Sound carried badly in this thin atmosphere.

"Desolate hole, if you ask me," said Ford. "I could have more fun in a cat litter." He felt a mounting irritation. Of all the planets in all the star systems of all the Galaxy—many wild and exotic, seething with life—didn't he just have to turn up at a dump like this after fifteen years of being a castaway? Not even a hot-dog stand in evidence. He stooped down and picked up a cold clod of earth, but there was nothing underneath it worth crossing thousands of light-years to look at.

"No," insisted Arthur, "don't you understand, this is the first time I've actually stood on the surface of another planet

. . . a whole alien world . . . ! Pity it's such a dump though."

Trillian hugged herself, shivered and frowned. She could have sworn she saw a slight and unexpected movement out of the corner of her eye, but when she glanced in that direction all she could see was the ship, still and silent, a hundred yards or so behind them.

She was relieved when a second or so later they caught sight of Zaphod standing on top of the ridge of ground and waving to them to come and join him.

He seemed to be excited, but they couldn't clearly hear what he was saying because of the thinnish atmosphere and the wind.

As they approached the ridge of higher ground they became aware that it seemed to be circular—a crater about a hundred and fifty yards wide. Round the outside of the crater the sloping ground was spattered with black and red lumps. They stopped and looked at a piece. It was wet. It was rubbery.

With horror they suddenly realized that it was fresh whalemeat.

At the top of the crater's lip they met Zaphod.

"Look," he said, pointing into the crater.

In the center lay the exploded carcass of a lonely sperm whale that hadn't lived long enough to be disappointed with its lot. The silence was only disturbed by the slight involuntary spasms of Trillian's throat.

"I suppose there's no point in trying to bury it?" murmured Arthur, and then wished he hadn't.

"Come," said Zaphod, and started back down into the crater.

"What, down there?" said Trillian with severe distaste.

"Yeah," said Zaphod, "come on, I've got something to show you."

"We can see it," said Trillian.

"Not that," said Zaphod, "something else. Come on."

They all hesitated.

"Come on," insisted Zaphod, "I've found a way in."

"*In?*" said Arthur in horror.

"Into the interior of the planet! An underground passage. The force of the whale's impact cracked it open, and that's where we have to go. Where no man has trod these five million years, into the very depths of time itself. . . ."

Marvin started his ironical humming again.

Zaphod hit him and he shut up.

With little shudders of disgust they all followed Zaphod down the incline into the crater, trying very hard to avoid looking at its unfortunate creator.

"Life," said Marvin dolefully, "loathe it or ignore it, you can't like it."

The ground had caved in where the whale had hit it, revealing a network of galleries and passages, now largely obstructed by collapsed rubble and entrails. Zaphod had made a start clearing a way into one of them, but Marvin was able to do it rather faster. Dank air wafted out of its dark recesses, and as Zaphod shone a flashlight into it, little was visible in the dusty gloom.

"According to the legends," he said, "the Magratheans lived most of their lives underground."

"Why's that?" said Arthur. "Did the surface become too polluted or overpopulated?"

"No, I don't think so," said Zaphod. "I think they just didn't like it very much."

"Are you sure you know what you're doing?" said Trillian, peering nervously into the darkness. "We've been attacked once already, you know."

"Look, kid, I promise you the live population of this planet is nil plus the four of us, so come on, let's get on in there. Er, hey, Earthman . . ."

"Arthur," said Arthur.

"Yeah, could you just sort of keep this robot with you and guard this end of the passageway. Okay?"

"Guard?" said Arthur. "What from? You just said there's no one here."

"Yeah, well, just for safety, okay?" said Zaphod.

"Whose? Yours or mine?"

"Good lad. Okay, here we go."

Zaphod scrambled down into the passage, followed by Trillian and Ford.

"Well, I hope you all have a really miserable time," complained Arthur.

"Don't worry," Marvin assured him, "they will."

In a few seconds they had disappeared from view.

Arthur stamped around in a huff, and then decided that a whale's graveyard is not on the whole a good place to stamp around in.

Marvin eyed him balefully for a moment, and then turned himself off.

Zaphod marched quickly down the passageway, nervous as hell, but trying to hide it by striding purposefully. He flung the beam around. The walls were covered in dark tiles and were cold to the touch, the air thick with decay.

"There, what did I tell you?" he said. "An inhabited

planet. Magrathea," and he strode on through the dirt and debris that littered the tile floors.

Trillian was reminded unavoidably of the London Underground, though it was less thoroughly squalid.

At intervals along the walls the tiles gave way to large mosaics—simple angular patterns in bright colors. Trillian stopped and studied one of them but could not interpret any sense in them. She called to Zaphod.

"Hey, have you any idea what these strange symbols are?"

"I think they're just strange symbols of some kind," said Zaphod, hardly glancing back.

Trillian shrugged and hurried after him.

From time to time a doorway led either to the left or right into smallish chambers which Ford discovered to be full of derelict computer equipment. He dragged Zaphod into one to have a look. Trillian followed.

"Look," said Ford, "you reckon this is Magrathea . . ."

"Yeah," said Zaphod, "and we heard the voice, right?"

"Okay, so I've bought the fact that it's Magrathea—for the moment. What you have so far said nothing about is how in the Galaxy you found it. You didn't just look it up in a star atlas, that's for sure."

"Research. Government archives. Detective work. Few lucky guesses. Easy."

"And then you stole the Heart of Gold to come and look for it with?"

"I stole it to look for a lot of things."

"A lot of things?" said Ford in surprise. "Like what?"

"I don't know."

"What?"

"I don't know what I'm looking for."

"Why not?"

"Because . . . because . . . I think it might be because if I knew I wouldn't be able to look for them."

"What, are you crazy?"

"It's a possibility I haven't ruled out yet," said Zaphod quietly. "I only know as much about myself as my mind can work out under its current conditions. And its current conditions are not good."

For a long time nobody said anything as Ford gazed at Zaphod with a mind suddenly full of worry.

"Listen, old friend, if you want to . . ." started Ford eventually.

"No, wait . . . I'll tell you something," said Zaphod. "I freewheel a lot. I get an idea to do something, and, hey, why not, I do it. I reckon I'll become President of the Galaxy, and it just happens, it's easy. I decide to steal this ship. I decide to look for Magrathea, and it all just happens. Yeah, I work out how it can best be done, right, but it always works out. It's like having a Galacticredit card which keeps on working though you never send off the checks. And then whenever I stop and think—why did I want to do something?—how did I work out how to do it?—I get a very strong desire just to stop thinking about it. Like I have now. It's a big effort to talk about it."

Zaphod paused for a while. For a while there was silence. Then he frowned and said, "Last night I was worrying about this again. About the fact that part of my mind just didn't seem to work properly. Then it occurred to me that the way it seemed was that someone else was using my mind to have good ideas with, without telling me about it. I put the two ideas together and decided that maybe that somebody had locked off part of my mind for that purpose, which was why I couldn't use it. I wondered if there was a way I could check.

"I went to the ship's medical bay and plugged myself into the encephalographic screen. I went through every major screening test on both my heads—all the tests I had to go through under Government medical officers before my nomination for presidency could be properly ratified. They showed up nothing. Nothing unexpected at least. They showed that I was clever, imaginative, irresponsible, untrustworthy, extrovert, nothing you couldn't have guessed. And no other anomalies. So I started inventing further tests, completely at random. Nothing. Then I tried superimposing the results from one head on top of the results from the other head. Still nothing. Finally I got silly, because I'd given it all up as nothing more than an attack of paranoia. Last thing I did before I packed it in was take the superimposed picture and look at it through a green filter. You remember I was always superstitious about the color green when I was a kid? I always wanted to be a pilot on one of the trading scouts?"

Ford nodded.

"And there it was," said Zaphod, "clear as day. A whole section in the middle of both brains that related only to each other and not to anything else around them. Some bastard had cauterized all the synapses and electronically traumatized those two lumps of cerebellum."

Ford stared at him, aghast. Trillian had turned white.

"Somebody *did* that to you?" whispered Ford.

"Yeah."

"But have you any idea who? Or why?"

"Why? I can only guess. But I do know who the bastard was."

"You know? How do you know?"

"Because they left their initials burned into the cauterized synapses. They left them there for me to see."

Ford stared at him in horror and felt his skin begin to crawl.

"Initials? Burned into your brain?"

"Yeah."

"Well, what were they, for God's sake?"

Zaphod looked at him in silence again for a moment. Then he looked away.

"Z.B.," he said quietly.

At that moment a steel shutter slammed down behind them and gas started to pour into the chamber.

"I'll tell you about it later," choked Zaphod as all three passed out.

Chapter 21

O n the surface of Magrathea Arthur wandered about moodily.

Ford had thoughtfully left him his copy of *The Hitchhiker's Guide to the Galaxy* to while away the time with. He pushed a few buttons at random.

The Hitchhiker's Guide to the Galaxy *is a very unevenly edited book and contains many passages that simply seemed to its editors like a good idea at the time.*

One of these (the one Arthur now came across) supposedly relates the experiences of one Veet Voojagig, a quiet young student at the University of Maximegalon, who pursued a brilliant academic career studying ancient philology, transformational ethics and the wave harmonic theory of historical perception, and then, after a night of drinking Pan Galactic Gargle Blasters with Zaphod Beeblebrox, became increasingly obsessed with the problem of what had happened to all the ballpoints he'd bought over the past few years.

There followed a long period of painstaking research during which he visited all the major centers of ballpoint loss throughout the Galaxy and eventually came up with a quaint little theory which quite caught the public imagination at the time. Somewhere in the cosmos, he said, along with all the planets inhabited by humanoids, reptiloids, fishoids, walking treeoids and superintelligent shades of the color blue, there was also a planet entirely given over to ballpoint life forms. And it was to this planet that unattended ballpoints would make their way, slipping away quietly through wormholes in space to a world where they knew they could enjoy a uniquely ballpoint-oid life-style, responding to highly ballpoint-oriented stimuli, and generally leading the ballpoint equivalent of the good life.

And as theories go this was all very fine and pleasant until Veet Voojagig suddenly claimed to have found this planet, and to have worked there for a while driving a limousine for a family of cheap green retractables, whereupon he was taken away, locked up, wrote a book and was finally sent into tax exile, which is the usual fate reserved for those who are determined to make fools of themselves in public.

When one day an expedition was sent to the spatial coordinates that Voojagig had claimed for this planet they discovered only a small asteroid inhabited by a solitary old man who claimed repeatedly that nothing was true, though he was later discovered to be lying.

There did, however, remain the question of both the mysterious sixty thousand Altairian dollars paid yearly into his Brantisvogan bank account, and of course Zaphod Beeblebrox's highly profitable secondhand ballpoint business.

Arthur read this, and put the book down.

The robot still sat there, completely inert.

Arthur got up and walked to the top of the crater. He walked around the crater. He watched two suns set magnificently over Magrathea.

He went back down into the crater. He woke the robot

up because even a manically depressed robot is better to talk to than nobody.

"Night's falling," he said. "Look, robot, the stars are coming out."

From the heart of a dark nebula it is possible to see very few stars, and only very faintly, but they were there to be seen.

The robot obediently looked at them, then looked back.

"I know," he said. "Wretched, isn't it?"

"But that sunset! I've never seen anything like it in my wildest dreams . . . the two suns! It was like mountains of fire boiling into space."

"I've seen it," said Marvin. "It's rubbish."

"We only ever had the one sun at home," persevered Arthur. "I came from a planet called Earth, you know."

"I know," said Marvin, "you keep going on about it. It sounds awful."

"Ah no, it was a beautiful place."

"Did it have oceans?"

"Oh yes," said Arthur with a sigh, "great wide rolling blue oceans . . ."

"Can't bear oceans," said Marvin.

"Tell me," inquired Arthur, "do you get on well with other robots?"

"Hate them," said Marvin. "Where are you going?"

Arthur couldn't bear any more. He had got up again.

"I think I'll just take another walk," he said.

"Don't blame you," said Marvin and counted five hundred and ninety-seven billion sheep before falling asleep again a second later.

Arthur slapped his arms about himself to try and get his circulation a little more enthusiastic about its job. He trudged back up the wall of the crater.

Because the atmosphere was so thin and because there was no moon, nightfall was very rapid and it was by now very dark. Because of this, Arthur practically walked into the old man before he noticed him.

Chapter 22

He was standing with his back to Arthur watching the very last glimmers of light sink into blackness behind the horizon. He was tallish, elderly and dressed in a single long gray robe. When he turned, his face was thin and distinguished, careworn but not unkind, the sort of face you would happily bank with. But he didn't turn yet, not even to react to Arthur's yelp of surprise.

Eventually the last rays of the sun vanished completely, and he turned. His face was still illuminated from somewhere, and when Arthur looked for the source of the light he saw that a few yards away stood a small craft of some kind—a small Hovercraft, Arthur guessed. It shed a dim pool of light around it.

The man looked at Arthur, sadly it seemed.

"You choose a cold night to visit our dead planet," he said.

"Who . . . who are you?" stammered Arthur.

The man looked away. Again a look of sadness seemed to cross his face.

"My name is not important," he said.

He seemed to have something on his mind. Conversation was clearly something he felt he didn't have to rush at. Arthur felt awkward.

"I . . . er . . . you startled me . . ." he said, lamely.

The man looked round to him again and slightly raised his eyebrows.

"Hmmm?" he said.

"I said you startled me."

"Do not be alarmed, I will not harm you."

Arthur frowned at him. "But you shot at us! There were missiles . . ." he said.

The man gazed into the pit of the crater. The slight glow from Marvin's eyes cast very faint red shadows on the huge carcass of the whale.

The man chuckled slightly.

"An automatic system," he said and gave a small sigh. "Ancient computers ranged in the bowels of the planet tick away the dark millennia, and the ages hang heavy on their dusty data banks. I think they take the occasional potshot to relieve the monotony."

He looked gravely at Arthur and said, "I'm a great fan of science, you know."

"Oh . . . er, really?" said Arthur, who was beginning to find the man's curious, kindly manner disconcerting.

"Oh yes," said the old man, and simply stopped talking again.

"Ah," said Arthur, "er . . ." He had an odd feeling of being like a man in the act of adultery who is surprised when the woman's husband wanders into the room, changes his trousers, passes a few idle remarks about the weather and leaves again.

"You seem ill at ease," said the old man with polite concern.

"Er, no . . . well, yes. Actually, you see, we weren't really expecting to find anybody about in fact. I sort of gathered that you were all dead or something . . ."

"Dead?" said the old man. "Good gracious me, no, we have but slept."

"Slept?" said Arthur incredulously.

"Yes, through the economic recession, you see," said the old man, apparently unconcerned about whether Arthur understood a word he was talking about or not.

Arthur had to prompt him again.

"Er, economic recession?"

"Well, you see, five million years ago the Galactic economy collapsed, and seeing that custom-built planets are something of a luxury commodity, you see . . ."

He puased and looked at Arthur.

"You know we built planets, do you?" he asked solemnly.

"Well, yes," said Arthur, "I'd sort of gathered . . ."

"Fascinating trade," said the old man, and a wistful look came into his eyes, "doing the coastlines was always my favorite. Used to have endless fun doing the little bits in fjords . . . so anyway," he said, trying to find his thread again, "the recession came and we decided it would save a lot of bother if we just slept through it. So we programmed the computers to revive us when it was all over."

The man stifled a very slight yawn and continued.

"The computers were index-linked to the Galactic stock-market prices, you see, so that we'd all be revived when everybody else had rebuilt the economy enough to afford our rather expensive services."

Arthur, a regular *Guardian* reader, was deeply shocked at this.

"That's a pretty unpleasant way to behave, isn't it?"

"Is it?" asked the old man mildly. "I'm sorry, I'm a bit out of touch."

He pointed down into the crater.

"Is that robot yours?" he said.

"No," came a thin metallic voice from the crater, "I'm mine."

"If you'd call it a robot," muttered Arthur. "It's more a sort of electronic sulking machine."

"Bring it," said the old man. Arthur was quite surprised to hear a note of decision suddenly present in the old man's voice. He called to Marvin, who crawled up the slope making a big show of being lame, which he wasn't.

"On second thoughts," said the old man, "leave it here. You must come with me. Great things are afoot." He turned toward his craft which, though no apparent signal had been given, now drifted quietly toward them through the dark.

Arthur looked down at Marvin, who now made an equally big show of turning round laboriously and trudging off down into the crater again muttering sour nothings to himself.

"Come," called the old man, "come now or you will be late."

"Late?" said Arthur. "What for?"

"What is your name, human?"

"Dent. Arthur Dent," said Arthur.

"Late, as in the late Dentarthurdent," said the old man, sternly. "It's a sort of threat, you see." Another wistful look came into his tired old eyes. "I've never been very good at them myself, but I'm told they can be very effective."

Arthur blinked at him.

"What an extraordinary person," he muttered to himself.

"I beg your pardon?" said the old man.

"Oh, nothing, I'm sorry," said Arthur in embarrassment. "All right, where do we go?"

"In my aircar," said the old man, motioning Arthur to get into the craft which had settled silently next to them. "We are going deep into the bowels of the planet where even now our race is being revived from its five-million-year slumber. Magrathea awakes."

Arthur shivered involuntarily as he seated himself next to the old man. The strangeness of it, the silent bobbing movement of the craft as it soared into the night sky, quite unsettled him.

He looked at the old man, his face illuminated by the dull glow of tiny lights on the instrument panel.

"Excuse me," he said to him, "what is your name, by the way?"

"My name?" said the old man, and the same distant sadness came into his face again. He paused. "My name," he said, "is Slartibartfast."

Arthur practically choked.

"I beg your pardon?" he spluttered.

"Slartibartfast," repeated the old man quietly.

"Slartibartfast?"

The old man looked at him gravely.

"I said it wasn't important," he said.

The aircar sailed through the night.

Chapter 23

I t is an important and popular fact that things are not always what they seem. For instance, on the planet Earth, man had always assumed that he was more intelligent than dolphins because he had achieved so much—the wheel, New York, wars and so on—while all the dolphins had ever done was muck about in the water having a good time. But conversely, the dolphins had always believed that they were far more intelligent than man—for precisely the same reasons.

Curiously enough, the dolphins had long known of the impending destruction of the planet Earth and had made many attempts to alert mankind to the danger; but most of their communications were misinterpreted as amusing attempts to punch footballs or whistle for tidbits, so they eventually gave up and left the Earth by their own means shortly before the Vogons arrived.

The last ever dolphin message was misinterpreted as a surprisingly sophisticated attempt to do a double-backward somersault through a hoop while whistling the "Star-Spangled Banner," but in fact the message was this: *So long and thanks for all the fish.*

In fact there was only one species on the planet more intelligent than dolphins, and they spent a lot of their time in behavioral research laboratories running round inside wheels and conducting frighteningly elegant and subtle experiments on man. The fact that once again man completely misinterpreted this relationship was entirely according to these creatures' plans.

Chapter 24

Silently the aircar coasted through the cold darkness, a single soft glow of light that was utterly alone in the deep Magrathean night. It sped swiftly. Arthur's companion seemed sunk in his own thoughts, and when Arthur tried on a couple of occasions to engage him in conversation again he would simply reply by asking if he was comfortable enough, and then left it at that.

Arthur tried to gauge the speed at which they were traveling, but the blackness outside was absolute and he was denied any reference points. The sense of motion was so soft and slight he could almost believe they were hardly moving at all.

Then a tiny glow of light appeared in the far distance and within seconds had grown so much in size that Arthur realized it was traveling toward them at a colossal speed, and he tried to make out what sort of craft it might be. He peered at it, but was unable to discern any clear shape, and suddenly gasped in alarm as the aircar dipped sharply and headed downward in what seemed certain to be a collision course. Their relative velocity seemed unbelievable, and Arthur had hardly time to draw breath before it was all over. The next thing he was aware of was an insane silver blur that seemed to surround him. He twisted his head sharply round and saw a small black point dwindling rapidly in the distance behind them, and it took him several seconds to realize what had happened.

They had plunged into a tunnel in the ground. The colossal speed had been their own, relative to the glow of light which was a stationary hole in the ground, the mouth of the tunnel. The insane blur of silver was the circular wall of the tunnel down which they were shooting, apparently at several hundred miles an hour.

He closed his eyes in terror.

After a length of time which he made no attempt to judge, he sensed a slight subsidence in their speed and some while later became aware that they were gradually gliding to a gentle halt.

He opened his eyes again. They were still in the silver tunnel, threading and weaving their way through what appeared to be a crisscross warren of converging tunnels. When they finally stopped it was in a small chamber of curved steel. Several tunnels also had their termini here, and at the farther end of the chamber Arthur could see a large circle of dim irritating light. It was irritating because it played tricks with the eyes, it was impossible to focus on it properly or tell how near or far it was. Arthur guessed (quite wrongly) that it might be ultraviolet.

Slartibartfast turned and regarded Arthur with his solemn old eyes.

"Earthman," he said, "we are now deep in the heart of Magrathea."

"How did you know I was an Earthman?" demanded Arthur.

"These things will become clear to you," said the old man gently, "at least," he added with slight doubt in his voice, "clearer than they are at the moment."

He continued: "I should warn you that the chamber we are about to pass into does not literally exist within our planet. It is a little too . . . large. We are about to pass through a gateway into a vast tract of hyperspace. It may disturb you."

Arthur made nervous noises.

Slartibartfast touched a button and added, not entirely reassuringly, "It scares the willies out of me. Hold tight."

The car shot forward straight into the circle of light, and suddenly Arthur had a fairly clear idea of what infinity looked like.

It wasn't infinity in fact. Infinity itself looks flat and uninteresting. Looking up into the night sky is looking into infinity—distance is incomprehensible and therefore meaningless. The chamber into which the aircar emerged was anything but infinite, it was just very very very big, so big that it gave the impression of infinity far better than infinity itself.

Arthur's senses bobbed and spun as, traveling at the immense speed he knew the aircar attained, they climbed slowly through the open air, leaving the gateway through which they had passed an invisible pinprick in the shimmering wall behind them.

The wall.

The wall defied the imagination—seduced it and defeated it. The wall was so paralyzingly vast and sheer that its top, bottom and sides passed away beyond the reach of sight. The mere shock of vertigo could kill a man.

The wall appeared perfectly flat. It would take the finest laser-measuring equipment to detect that as it climbed, apparently to infinity, as it dropped dizzily away, as it planed out to either side, it also curved. It met itself again thirteen light seconds away. In other words the wall formed the inside of a hollow sphere, a sphere over three million miles across and flooded with unimaginable light.

"Welcome," said Slartibartfast as the tiny speck that was the aircar, traveling now at three times the speed of sound, crept imperceptibly forward into the mind-boggling space, "welcome," he said, "to our factory floor."

Arthur stared about him in a kind of wonderful horror. Ranged away before them, at distances he could neither judge nor even guess at, were a series of curious suspensions, delicate traceries of metal and light hung about shadowy spherical shapes that hung in the space.

"This," said Slartibartfast, "is where we make most of our planets, you see."

"You mean," said Arthur, trying to form the words, "you mean you're starting it all up again now?"

"No no, good heavens, no," exclaimed the old man, "no, the Galaxy isn't nearly rich enough to support us yet. No, we've been awakened to perform just one extraordinary commission for very . . . special clients from another dimension. It may interest you . . . there in the distance in front of us."

Arthur followed the old man's finger till he was able to pick out the floating structure he was pointing out. It was indeed the only one of the many structures that betrayed any sign of activity about it, though this was more a subliminal impression than anything one could put one's finger on.

At that moment, however, a flash of light arced through the structure and revealed in stark relief the patterns that were formed on the dark sphere within. Patterns that Arthur knew, rough blobby shapes that were as familiar to him as the shapes of words, part of the furniture of his mind. For a few seconds he sat in stunned silence as the images rushed around his mind and tried to find somewhere to settle down and make sense.

Part of his brain told him that he knew perfectly well what he was looking at and what the shapes represented while another quite sensibly refused to countenance the idea and abdicated responsibility for any further thinking in that direction.

The flash came again, and this time there could be no doubt.

"The Earth . . ." whispered Arthur.

"Well, the Earth Mark Two in fact," said Slartibartfast cheerfully. "We're making a copy from our original blueprints."

There was a pause.

"Are you trying to tell me," said Arthur, slowly and with control, "that you originally . . . *made* the Earth?"

"Oh yes," said Slartibartfast. "Did you ever go to a place . . . I think it was called Norway?"

"No," said Arthur, "no, I didn't."

"Pity," said Slartibartfast, "that was one of mine. Won an award, you know. Lovely crinkly edges. I was most upset to hear of its destruction."

"*You* were upset!"

"Yes. Five minutes later and it wouldn't have mattered so much. It was a quite shocking cock-up."

"Huh?" said Arthur.

"The mice were furious."

"The *mice* were furious?"

"Oh yes," said the old man mildly.

"Yes, well, so I expect were the dogs and cats and duck-billed platypuses, but . . ."

"Ah, but they hadn't paid for it, you see, had they?"

"Look," said Arthur, "would it save you a lot of time if I just gave up and went mad now?"

For a while the aircar flew on in awkward silence. Then the old man tried patiently to explain.

"Earthman, the planet you lived on was commissioned, paid for, and run by mice. It was destroyed five minutes before the completion of the purpose for which it was built, and we've got to build another one."

Only one word was registering with Arthur.

"*Mice?*" he said.

"Indeed, Earthman."

"Look, sorry, are we talking about the little white furry things with the cheese fixation and women standing on tables screaming in early sixties sitcoms?"

Slartibartfast coughed politely.

"Earthman," he said, "it is sometimes hard to follow your mode of speech. Remember I have been asleep inside this planet of Magrathea for five million years and know little of these early sixties sitcoms of which you speak. These creatures you call mice, you see, they are not quite as they appear. They are merely the protrusion into our dimension of vastly hyperintelligent pandimensional beings. The whole business with the cheese and the squeaking is just a front."

The old man paused, and with a sympathetic frown continued. "They've been experimenting on you, I'm afraid."

Arthur thought about this for a second, and then his face cleared.

"Ah no," he said, "I see the source of the misunderstanding now. No, look, you see what happened was that we used to do experiments on *them*. They were often used in behavioral research, Pavlov and all that sort of stuff. So what happened was that the mice would be set all sorts of tests, learning to ring bells, run round mazes and things so that the whole nature of the learning process could be examined. From our observations of their behavior we were able to learn all sorts of things about our own. . . ."

Arthur's voice trailed off.

"Such subtlety. . ." said Slartibartfast, "one has to admire it."

"What?" said Arthur.

"How better to disguise their real natures, and how better to guide your thinking. Suddenly running down a maze the wrong way, eating the wrong bit of cheese, unexpectedly dropping dead of myxomatosis. If it's finely calculated the cumulative effect is enormous."

He paused for effect.

"You see, Earthman, they really are particularly clever hyperintelligent pandimensional beings. Your planet and people have formed the matrix of an organic computer running a ten-million-year research program. . . . Let me tell you the whole story. It'll take a little time."

"Time," said Arthur weakly, "is not currently one of my problems."

Chapter 25

There are of course many problems connected with life, of which some of the most popular are *Why are people born? Why do they die? Why do they want to spend so much of the intervening time wearing digital watches?*

Many many millions of years ago a race of hyperintelligent pandimensional beings (whose physical manifestation in their own pandimensional universe is not dissimilar to our own) got so fed up with the constant bickering about the meaning of life which used to interrupt their favorite pastime of Brockian Ultra Cricket (a curious game which involved suddenly hitting people for no readily apparent reason and then running away) that they decided to sit down and solve their problems once and for all.

And to this end they built themselves a stupendous super computer which was so amazingly intelligent that even before its data banks had been connected up it had started from *I think therefore I am* and got as far as deducing the existence of rice pudding and income tax before anyone managed to turn it off.

It was the size of a small city.

Its main console was installed in a specially designed executive office, mounted on an enormous executive desk of finest ultramahogany topped with rich ultrared leather. The dark carpeting was discreetly sumptuous, exotic pot plants and tastefully engraved prints of the principal computer programmers and their families were deployed liberally about the room, and stately windows looked out upon a tree-lined public square.

On the day of the Great On-Turning two soberly dressed programmers with briefcases arrived and were shown discreetly into the office. They were aware that this day they would represent their entire race in its greatest moment, but they conducted themselves calmly and quietly as they seated themselves deferentially before the desk, opened their briefcases and took out their leather-bound notebooks.

Their names were Lunkwill and Fook.

For a few moments they sat in respectful silence, then, after exchanging a quiet glance with Fook, Lunkwill leaned forward and touched a small black panel.

The subtlest of hums indicated that the massive computer was now in total active mode. After a pause it spoke to them in a voice rich, resonant and deep.

It said: "What is this great task for which I, Deep Thought, the second greatest computer in the Universe of Time and Space, have been called into existence?"

Lunkwill and Fook glanced at each other in surprise.

"Your task, O computer . . ." began Fook.

"No, wait a minute, this isn't right," said Lunkwill, worried. "We distinctly designed this computer to be the greatest one ever and we're not making do with second best.

Deep Thought," he addressed the computer, "are you not as we designed you to be, the greatest, most powerful computer in all time?"

"I described myself as the second greatest," intoned Deep Thought, "and such I am."

Another worried look passed between the two programmers. Lunkwill cleared his throat.

"There must be some mistake," he said, "are you not a greater computer than the Milliard Gargantubrain at Maximegalon which can count all the atoms in a star in a millisecond?"

"The Milliard Gargantubrain?" said Deep Thought with unconcealed contempt. "A mere abacus—mention it not."

"And are you not," said Fook leaning anxiously forward, "a greater analyst than the Googleplex Star Thinker in the Seventh Galaxy of Light and Ingenuity which can calculate the trajectory of every single dust particle throughout a five-week Dangrabad Beta sand blizzard?"

"A five-week sand blizzard?" said Deep Thought haughtily. "You ask this of me who have contemplated the very vectors of the atoms in the Big Bang itself? Molest me not with this pocket calculator stuff."

The two programmers sat in uncomfortable silence for a moment. Then Lunkwill leaned forward again.

"But are you not," he said, "a more fiendish disputant than the Great Hyperlobic Omni-Cognate Neutron Wrangler of Ciceronicus Twelve, the Magic and Indefatigable?"

"The Great Hyperlobic Omni-Cognate Neutron Wrangler," said Deep Thought, thoroughly rolling the *r*'s, "could talk all four legs off an Arcturan Mega-Donkey—but only I could persuade it to go for a walk afterward."

"Then what," asked Fook, "is the problem?"

"There is no problem," said Deep Thought with magnificent ringing tones. "I am simply the second greatest computer in the Universe of Space and Time."

"But the *second?*" insisted Lunkwill. "Why do you keep saying the second? You're surely not thinking of the Multicorticoid Perspicutron Titan Muller, are you? Or the Pondermatic? Or the . . ."

Contemptuous lights flashed across the computer's console.

"I spare not a single unit of thought on these cybernetic simpletons!" he boomed. "I speak of none but the computer that is to come after me!"

Fook was losing patience. He pushed his notebook aside and muttered, "I think this is getting needlessly messianic."

"You know nothing of future time," pronounced Deep Thought, "and yet in my teeming circuitry I can navigate the infinite delta streams of future probability and see that there must one day come a computer whose merest operational parameters I am not worthy to calculate, but which it will be my fate eventually to design."

Fook sighed heavily and glanced across to Lunkwill.

"Can we get on and ask the question?" he said.

Lunkwill motioned him to wait.

"What computer is this of which you speak?" he asked.

"I will speak of it no further in this present time," said Deep Thought. "Now. Ask what else of me you will that I may function. Speak."

They shrugged at each other. Fook composed himself.

"O Deep Thought computer," he said, "the task we have designed you to perform is this. We want you to tell us . . ." he paused, "the Answer!"

"The Answer?" said Deep Thought. "The Answer to what?"

"Life!" urged Fook.

"The Universe!" said Lunkwill.

"Everything!" they said in chorus.

Deep Thought paused for a moment's reflection.

"Tricky," he said finally.

"But can you do it?"

Again, a significant pause.

"Yes," said Deep Thought, "I can do it."

"There is an answer?" said Fook with breathless excitement.

"A simple answer?" added Lunkwill.

"Yes," said Deep Thought. "Life, the Universe, and Everything. There is an answer. But," he added, "I'll have to think about it."

A sudden commotion destroyed the moment: the door flew open and two angry men wearing the coarse faded-blue robes and belts of the Cruxwan University burst into the room, thrusting aside the ineffectual flunkie who tried to bar their way.

"We demand admission!" shouted the younger of the two men elbowing a pretty young secretary in the throat.

"Come on," shouted the older one, "you can't keep us out!" He pushed a junior programmer back through the door.

"We demand that you can't keep us out!" bawled the younger one, though he was now firmly inside the room and no further attempts were being made to stop him.

"Who are you?" said Lunkwill, rising angrily from his seat. "What do you want?"

"I am Majikthise!" announced the older one.

"And I demand that I am Vroomfondel!" shouted the younger one.

Majikthise turned on Vroomfondel. "It's all right," he explained angrily, "you don't need to demand that."

"All right!" bawled Vroomfondel, banging on a nearby desk. "I am Vroomfondel, and that is *not* a demand, that is a solid *fact!* What we demand is solid *facts!*"

"No, we don't!" exclaimed Majikthise in irritation. "That is precisely what we don't demand!"

Scarcely pausing for breath, Vroomfondel shouted, "We *don't* demand solid facts! What we demand is a total *absence* of solid facts. I demand that I may or may not be Vroomfondel!"

"But who the devil are you?" exclaimed an outraged Fook.

"We," said Majikthise, "are Philosophers."

"Though we may not be," said Vroomfondel, waving a warning finger at the programmers.

"Yes, we *are*," insisted Majikthise. "We are quite definitely here as representatives of the Amalgamated Union of Philosophers, Sages, Luminaries and Other Thinking Persons, and we want this machine off, and we want it off *now!*"

"What's the problem?" said Lunkwill.

"I'll tell you what the problem is, mate," said Majikthise, "demarcation, that's the problem!"

"We demand," yelled Vroomfondel, "that demarcation may or may not be the problem!"

"You just let the machines get on with the adding up," warned Majikthise, "and we'll take care of the eternal verities, thank you very much. You want to check your legal position, you do, mate. Under law the Quest for Ultimate Truth is quite clearly the inalienable prerogative of your working thinkers. Any bloody machine goes and actually *finds* it and we're straight out of a job, aren't we? I mean, what's the use of our sitting up half the night arguing that there may or may not be a God if this machine only goes and gives you his bleeding phone number the next morning?"

"That's right," shouted Vroomfondel, "we demand rigidly defined areas of doubt and uncertainty!"

Suddenly a stentorian voice boomed across the room.

"Might *I* make an observation at this point?" inquired Deep Thought.

"We'll go on strike!" yelled Vroomfondel.

"That's right!" agreed Majikthise. "You'll have a national Philosophers' strike on your hands!"

The hum level in the room suddenly increased as several ancillary bass driver units, mounted in sedately carved and varnished cabinet speakers around the room, cut in to give Deep Thought's voice a little more power.

"All I wanted to say," bellowed the computer, "is that my circuits are now irrevocably committed to calculating the answer to the Ultimate Question of Life, the Universe, and Everything." He paused and satisfied himself that he now had everyone's attention, before continuing more quietly. "But the program will take me a little while to run."

Fook glanced impatiently at his watch.

"How long?" he said.

"Seven and a half million years," said Deep Thought.

Lunkwill and Fook blinked at each other.

"Seven and a half million years!" they cried in chorus.

"Yes," declaimed Deep Thought, "I said I'd have to think about it, didn't I? And it occurs to me that running a program like this is bound to create an enormous amount of popular publicity for the whole area of philosophy in general. Everyone's going to have their own theories about what answer I'm eventually going to come up with, and who better to capitalize on that media market than you yourselves? So long as you can keep disagreeing with each other violently enough and maligning each other in the popular press, and so long as you have clever agents, you can keep yourselves on the gravy train for life. How does that sound?"

The two philosophers gaped at him.

"Bloody hell," said Majikthise, "now that is what I call thinking. Here, Vroomfondel, why do we never think of things like that?"

"Dunno," said Vroomfondel in an awed whisper; "think our brains must be too highly trained, Majikthise."

So saying, they turned on their heels and walked out of the door and into a life-style beyond their wildest dreams.

Chapter 26

Yes, very salutary," said Arthur, after Slartibartfast had related the salient points of this story to him, "but I don't understand what all this has got to do with the Earth and mice and things."

"That is but the first half of the story, Earthman," said the old man. "If you would care to discover what happened seven and a half million years later, on the great day of the Answer, allow me to invite you to my study where you can experience the events yourself on our Sens-O-Tape records. That is, unless you would care to take a quick stroll on the surface of New Earth. It's only half completed, I'm afraid—we haven't even finished burying the artificial dinosaur skeletons in the crust yet, then we have the Tertiary and Quaternary Periods of the Cenozoic Era to lay down, and . . ."

"No, thank you," said Arthur, "it wouldn't be quite the same."

"No," said Slartibartfast, "it won't be," and he turned the aircar round and headed back toward the mind-numbing wall.

lartibartfast's study was a total mess, like the results of an explosion in a public library. The old
man frowned as they stepped in.

"Terribly unfortunate," he said, "a diode
blew in one of the life-support computers. When we tried
to revive our cleaning staff we discovered they'd been dead
for nearly thirty thousand years. Who's going to clear away
the bodies, that's what I want to know. Look, why don't
you sit yourself down over there and let me plug you in?"

He gestured Arthur toward a chair which looked as if it
had been made out of the rib cage of a stegosaurus.

"It was made out of the rib cage of a stegosaurus," explained the old man as he pottered about fishing bits of wire
out from under tottering piles of paper and drawing instruments. "Here," he said, "hold these," and passed a couple of
stripped wire ends to Arthur.

The instant he took hold of them a bird flew straight
through him.

He was suspended in midair and totally invisible to himself. Beneath him was a pretty tree-lined city square, and all
around it as far as the eye could see were white concrete
buildings of airy spacious design but somewhat the worse
for wear--many were cracked and stained with rain. Today, however, the sun was shining, a fresh breeze danced

lightly through the trees, and the odd sensation that all the buildings were quietly humming was probably caused by the fact that the square and all the streets around it were thronged with cheerful excited people. Somewhere a band was playing, brightly colored flags were fluttering in the breeze and the spirit of carnival was in the air.

Arthur felt extraordinarily lonely stuck up in the air above it all without so much as a body to his name, but before he had time to reflect on this a voice rang out across the square and called for everyone's attention.

A man standing on a brightly dressed dais before the building which clearly dominated the square was addressing the crowd over a tannoy.

"O people who wait in the shadow of Deep Thought!" he cried out. "Honored Descendants of Vroomfondel and Majikthise, the Greatest and Most Truly Interesting Pundits the Universe has ever known, the Time of Waiting is over!"

Wild cheers broke out among the crowd. Flags, streamers and wolf whistles sailed through the air. The narrower streets looked rather like centipedes rolled over on their backs and frantically waving their legs in the air.

"Seven and a half million years our race has waited for this Great and Hopefully Enlightening Day!" cried the cheerleader. "The Day of the Answer!"

Hurrahs burst from the ecstatic crowd.

"Never again," cried the man, "never again will we wake up in the morning and think *Who am I? What is my purpose in life? Does it really, cosmically speaking*, matter *if I don't get up and go to work?* For today we will finally learn once and for all the plain and simple answer to all these nagging little problems of Life, the Universe and Everything!"

As the crowd erupted once again, Arthur found himself gliding through the air and down toward one of the large stately windows on the first floor of the building behind the dais from which the speaker was addressing the crowd.

He experienced a moment's panic as he sailed straight toward the window, which passed when a second or so later he found he had gone right through the solid glass without apparently touching it.

No one in the room remarked on his peculiar arrival, which is hardly surprising as he wasn't there. He began to realize that the whole experience was merely a recorded projection which knocked six-track seventy-millimeter into a cocked hat.

The room was much as Slartibartfast had described it. In seven and a half million years it had been well looked after and cleaned regularly every century or so. The ultra-mahogany desk was worn at the edges, the carpet a little faded now, but the large computer terminal sat in sparkling glory on the desk's leather top, as bright as if it had been constructed yesterday.

Two severely dressed men sat respectfully before the terminal and waited.

"The time is nearly upon us," said one, and Arthur was surprised to see a word suddenly materialize in thin air just by the man's neck. The word was LOONQUAWL, and it flashed a couple of times and then disappeared again. Before Arthur was able to assimilate this the other man spoke and the word PHOUCHG appeared by his neck.

"Seventy-five thousand generations ago, our ancestors set this program in motion," the second man said, "and in all that time we will be the first to hear the computer speak."

"An awesome prospect, Phouchg," agreed the first man, and Arthur suddenly realized he was watching a recording with subtitles.

"We are the ones who will hear," said Phouchg, "the answer to the great question of Life . . . !"

"The Universe . . . !" said Loonquawl.

"And Everything . . . !"

"Shhh," said Loonquawl with a slight gesture, "I think Deep Thought is preparing to speak!"

There was a moment's expectant pause while panels slowly came to life on the front of the console. Lights flashed on and off experimentally and settled down into a businesslike pattern. A soft low hum came from the communication channel.

"Good morning," said Deep Thought at last.

"Er . . . good morning, O Deep Thought," said Loonquawl nervously, "do you have . . . er, that is . . ."

"An answer for you?" interrupted Deep Thought majestically. "Yes. I have."

The two men shivered with expectancy. Their waiting had not been in vain.

"There really is one?" breathed Phouchg.

"There really is one," confirmed Deep Thought.

"To Everything? To the great Question of Life, the Universe and Everything?"

"Yes."

Both of the men had been trained for this moment, their lives had been a preparation for it, they had been selected at birth as those who would witness the answer, but even so they found themselves gasping and squirming like excited children.

"And you're ready to give it to us?" urged Loonquawl.

"I am."

"Now?"

"Now," said Deep Thought.

They both licked their dry lips.

"Though I don't think," added Deep Thought, "that you're going to like it."

"Doesn't matter!" said Phouchg. "We must know it! Now!"

"Now?" inquired Deep Thought.

"Yes! Now . . ."

"All right," said the computer, and settled into silence again. The two men fidgeted. The tension was unbearable.

"You're really not going to like it," observed Deep Thought.

"Tell us!"

"All right," said Deep Thought. "The Answer to the Great Question . . ."

"Yes . . . !"

"Of Life, the Universe and Everything . . ." said Deep Thought.

"Yes . . . !"

"Is . . ." said Deep Thought, and paused.

"Yes . . . !"

"Is . . ."

"Yes . . . !!! . . . ?"

"Forty-two," said Deep Thought, with infinite majesty and calm.

Chapter 28

I t was a long long time before anyone spoke.

Out of the corner of his eye Phouchg could see the sea of tense expectant faces down in the square outside.

"We're going to get lynched, aren't we?" he whispered.

"It was a tough assignment," said Deep Thought mildly.

"Forty-two!" yelled Loonquawl. "Is that all you've got to show for seven and a half million years' work?"

"I checked it very thoroughly," said the computer, "and that quite definitely is the answer. I think the problem, to be quite honest with you, is that you've never actually known what the question is."

"But it was the Great Question! The Ultimate Question of Life, the Universe and Everything," howled Loonquawl.

"Yes," said Deep Thought with the air of one who suffers fools gladly, "but what actually *is* it?"

A slow stupefied silence crept over the men as they stared at the computer and then at each other.

"Well, you know, it's just Everything . . . everything . . ." offered Phouchg weakly.

"Exactly!" said Deep Thought. "So once you do know what the question actually is, you'll know what the answer means."

"Oh, terrific," muttered Phouchg, flinging aside his notebook and wiping away a tiny tear.

"Look, all right, all right," said Loonquawl, "can you just please *tell* us the question?"

"The Ultimate Question?"

"Yes!"

"Of Life, the Universe and Everything?"

"Yes!"

Deep Thought pondered for a moment.

"Tricky," he said.

"But can you do it?" cried Loonquawl.

Deep Thought pondered this for another long moment.

Finally: "No," he said firmly.

Both men collapsed onto their chairs in despair.

"But I'll tell you who can," said Deep Thought.

They both looked up sharply.

"Who? Tell us!"

Suddenly Arthur began to feel his apparently nonexistent scalp begin to crawl as he found himself moving slowly but inexorably forward toward the console, but it was only a dramatic zoom on the part of whoever had made the recording, he assumed.

"I speak of none but the computer that is to come after me," intoned Deep Thought, his voice regaining its accustomed declamatory tones. "A computer whose merest operational parameters I am not worthy to calculate—and yet I will design it for you. A computer that can calculate the Question to the Ultimate Answer, a computer of such infinite and subtle complexity that organic life itself shall form part of its operational matrix. And you yourselves shall take on new forms and go down into the computer to navigate its ten-million-year program! Yes! I shall design this computer for you. And I shall name it also unto you. And it shall be called . . . the Earth."

Phouchg gaped at Deep Thought.

"What a dull name," he said, and great incisions appeared down the length of his body. Loonquawl too suddenly sustained horrific gashes from nowhere. The Computer console blotched and cracked, the walls flickered and crumbled and the room crashed upward into its own ceiling. . . .

Slartibartfast was standing in front of Arthur holding the two wires.

"End of the tape," he explained.

Chapter 29

Zaphod! Wake up!"

"Mmmmmwwwwwwerrrr?"

"Hey, come on, wake up."

"Just let me stick to what I'm good at, yeah?" muttered Zaphod, and rolled away from the voice back to sleep.

"Do you want me to kick you?" said Ford.

"Would it give you a lot of pleasure?" said Zaphod, blearily.

"No."

"Nor me. So what's the point? Stop bugging me." Zaphod curled himself up.

"He got a double dose of the gas," said Trillian, looking down at him, "two windpipes."

"And stop talking," said Zaphod, "it's hard enough trying to sleep anyway. What's the matter with the ground? It's all cold and hard."

"It's gold," said Ford.

With an amazingly balletic movement Zaphod was standing and scanning the horizon, because that was how far the gold ground stretched in every direction, perfectly smooth and solid. It gleamed like . . . it's impossible to say what it gleamed like because nothing in the Universe gleams in quite the same way that a planet made of solid gold does.

"Who put all that there?" yelped Zaphod, goggle-eyed.

"Don't get excited," said Ford, "it's only a catalog."

"A who?"

"A catalog," said Trillian, "an illusion."

"How can you say that?" cried Zaphod, falling to his hands and knees and staring at the ground. He poked it and prodded it. It was very heavy and very slightly soft—he could mark it with his fingernail. It was very yellow and very shiny, and when he breathed on it his breath evaporated off it in that very peculiar and special way that breath evaporates off solid gold.

"Trillian and I came round a while ago," said Ford. "We shouted and yelled till somebody came and then carried on shouting and yelling till they got fed up and put us in their planet catalog to keep us busy till they were ready to deal with us. This is all Sens-O-Tape."

Zaphod stared at him bitterly.

"Ah, shit," he said, "you wake me up from my own perfectly good dream to show me somebody else's." He sat down in a huff.

"What's that series of valleys over there?" he said.

"Hallmark," said Ford. "We had a look."

"We didn't wake you earlier," said Trillian. "The last planet was knee-deep in fish."

"Fish?"

"Some people like the oddest things."

"And before that," said Ford, "we had platinum. Bit dull. We thought you'd like to see this one though."

Seas of light glared at them in one solid blaze wherever they looked.

"Very pretty," said Zaphod petulantly.

In the sky a huge green catalog number appeared. It flickered and changed, and when they looked around again so had the land.

As with one voice they all went, "Yuch."

The sea was purple. The beach they were on was composed of tiny yellow and green pebbles, presumably terribly precious stones. The mountains in the distance seemed soft and undulating with red peaks. Nearby stood a solid silver beach table with a frilly mauve parasol and silver tassles.

In the sky a huge sign appeared, replacing the catalog number. It said, *Whatever your tastes, Magrathea can cater for you. We are not proud.*

And five hundred entirely naked women dropped out of the sky on parachutes.

In a moment the scene vanished and left them in a springtime meadow full of cows.

"Ow!" said Zaphod. "My brains!"

"You want to talk about it?" said Ford.

"Yeah, okay," said Zaphod, and all three sat down and ignored the scenes that came and went around them.

"I figure this," said Zaphod. "Whatever happened to my mind, I did it. And I did it in such a way that it wouldn't be detected by the Government screening tests. And I wasn't to know anything about it myself. Pretty crazy, right?"

The other two nodded in agreement.

"So I reckon, what's so secret that I can't let anybody know I know it, not the Galactic Government, not even myself? And the answer is I don't know. Obviously. But I put a few things together and I can begin to guess. When did I decide to run for President? Shortly after the death of President Yooden Vranx. You remember Yooden, Ford?"

"Yeah," said Ford, "he was that guy we met when we were kids, the Arcturan captain. He was a gas. He gave us conkers when you bust your way into his megafreighter. Said you were the most amazing kid he'd ever met."

"What's all this?" said Trillian.

"Ancient history," said Ford, "when we were kids together on Betelgeuse. The Arcturan megafreighters used to carry most of the bulky trade between the Galactic Center and the outlying regions. The Betelgeuse trading scouts used to find the markets and the Arcturans would supply them. There was a lot of trouble with space pirates before they were wiped out in the Dordellis wars, and the megafreighters had to be equipped with the most fantastic defense shields known to Galactic science. They were real brutes of ships, and huge. In orbit round a planet they would eclipse the sun.

"One day, young Zaphod here decides to raid one. On a trijet scooter designed for stratosphere work, a mere kid. I mean forget it, it was crazier than a mad monkey. I went along for the ride because I'd got some very safe money on him not doing it, and didn't want him coming back with fake evidence. So what happens? We get in his trijet which he had souped up into something totally other, crossed three parsecs in a matter of weeks, bust our way into a mega-freighter I still don't know how, marched on to the bridge waving toy pistols and demanded conkers. A wilder thing I have not known. Lost me a year's pocket money. For what? Conkers."

"The captain was this really amazing guy, Yooden Vranx," said Zaphod. "He gave us food, booze—stuff from really weird parts of the Galaxy—lots of conkers, of course, and we had just the most incredible time. Then he tele-ported us back. Into the maximum security wing of the Betelgeuse state prison. He was a cool guy. Went on to become President of the Galaxy."

Zaphod paused.

The scene around them was currently plunged into gloom. Dark mists swirled round them and elephantine shapes lurked indistinctly in the shadows. The air was occasionally rent with the sounds of illusory beings murdering other illusory beings. Presumably enough people must have liked this sort of thing to make it a paying proposition.

"Ford," said Zaphod quietly.

"Yeah?"

"Just before Yooden died he came to see me."

"What? You never told me."

"No."

"What did he say? What did he come to see you about?"

"He told me about the Heart of Gold. It was his idea that I should steal it."

"*His* idea?"

"Yeah," said Zaphod, "and the only possible way of stealing it was to be at the launching ceremony."

Ford gaped at him in astonishment for a moment, and then roared with laughter.

"Are you telling me," he said, "that you set yourself up to become President of the Galaxy just to steal that ship?"

"That's it," said Zaphod with the sort of grin that would get most people locked away in a room with soft walls.

"But why?" said Ford. "What's so important about having it?"

"Dunno," said Zaphod. "I think if I'd consciously known what was so important about it and what I would need it for it would have showed up on the brain screening tests and I would never have passed. I think Yooden told me a lot of things that are still locked away."

"So you think you went and mucked about inside your own brain as a result of Yooden talking to you?"

"He was a hell of a talker."

"Yeah, but Zaphod, old mate, you want to look after yourself, you know."

Zaphod shrugged.

"I mean, don't you have any inkling of the reasons for all this?" asked Ford.

Zaphod thought hard about this and doubts seemed to cross his mind.

"No," he said at last, "I don't seem to be letting myself into any of my secrets. Still," he added on further reflection, "I can understand that. I wouldn't trust myself further than I could spit a rat."

A moment later, the last planet in the catalog vanished from beneath them and the solid world resolved itself again.

They were sitting in a plush waiting room full of glass-top tables and design awards.

A tall Magrathean man was standing in front of them. "The mice will see you now," he said.

Chapter 30

So there you have it," said Slartibartfast, making a feeble and perfunctory attempt to clear away some of the appalling mess of his study. He picked up a piece of paper from the top of a pile, but then couldn't think of anywhere else to put it, so he put it back on top of the original pile which promptly fell over. "Deep Thought designed the Earth, we built it and you lived on it."

"And the Vogons came and destroyed it five minutes before the program was completed," added Arthur, not unbitterly. "Yes," said the old man, pausing to gaze hopelessly round the room. "Ten million years of planning and work gone just like that. Ten million years, Earthman, can you conceive of that kind of time span? A galactic civilization could grow from a single worm five times over in that time. Gone." He paused. "Well, that's bureaucracy for you," he added.

"You know," said Arthur thoughtfully, "all this explains a lot of things. All through my life I've had this strange unaccountable feeling that something was going on in the world, something big, even sinister, and no one would tell me what it was."

"No," said the old man, "that's just perfectly normal paranoia. Everyone in the Universe has that."

"Everyone?" said Arthur. "Well, if everyone has that perhaps it means something! Perhaps somewhere outside the Universe we know . . ."

"Maybe. Who cares?" said Slartibartfast before Arthur got too excited. "Perhaps I'm old and tired," he continued, "but I always think that the chances of finding out what really is going on are so absurdly remote that the only thing to do is to say hang the sense of it and just keep yourself occupied. Look at me: I design coastlines. I got an award for Norway."

He rummaged around in a pile of debris and pulled out a large Plexiglas block with his name on it and a model of Norway molded into it.

"Where's the sense in that?" he said. "None that I've been able to make out. I've been doing fjords all my life. For a fleeting moment they become fashionable and I get a major award."

He turned it over in his hands with a shrug and tossed it aside carelessly, but not so carelessly that it didn't land on something soft.

"In this replacement Earth we're building they've given me Africa to do and of course I'm doing it with all fjords again because I happen to like them, and I'm old-fashioned enough to think that they give a lovely baroque feel to a continent. And they tell me it's not equatorial enough. Equatorial!" He gave a hollow laugh. "What does it matter? Science has achieved some wonderful things, of course, but I'd far rather be happy than right any day."

"And are you?"

"No. That's where it all falls down, of course."

"Pity," said Arthur with sympathy. "It sounded like quite a good life-style otherwise."

Somewhere on the wall a small white light flashed.

"Come," said Slartibartfast, "you are to meet the mice. Your arrival on the planet has caused considerable excitement. It has already been hailed, so I gather, as the third most improbable event in the history of the Universe."

"What were the first two?"

"Oh, probably just coincidences," said Slartibartfast carelessly. He opened the door and stood waiting for Arthur to follow.

Arthur glanced around him once more, and then down at himself, at the sweaty disheveled clothes he had been lying in the mud in on Thursday morning.

"I seem to be having tremendous difficulty with my life-style," he muttered to himself.

"I beg your pardon?" asked the old man mildly.

"Oh, nothing," said Arthur, "only joking."

t is of course well known that careless talk costs
lives, but the full scale of the problem is not always
appreciated.

For instance, at the very moment that Arthur said,
"I seem to be having tremendous difficulty with my life-
style," a freak wormhole opened up in the fabric of the
space-time continuum and carried his words far far back in
time across almost infinite reaches of space to a distant Galaxy where strange and warlike beings were poised on the
brink of frightful interstellar battle.

The two opposing leaders were meeting for the last time.

A dreadful silence fell across the conference table as the
commander of the Vl'hurgs, resplendent in his black jeweled battle shorts, gazed levelly at the G'Gugvuntt leader
squatting opposite him in a cloud of green sweet-smelling
steam, and, with a million sleek and horribly beweaponed
star cruisers poised to unleash electric death at his single
word of command, challenged the vile creature to take back
what it had said about his mother.

The creature stirred in his sickly broiling vapor, and at
that very moment the words *I seem to be having tremendous
difficulty with my life-style* drifted across the conference
table.

Unfortunately, in the Vl'Hurg tongue this was the most

dreadful insult imaginable, and there was nothing for it but to wage terrible war for centuries.

Eventually, of course, after their Galaxy had been decimated over a few thousand years, it was realized that the whole thing had been a ghastly mistake, and so the two opposing battle fleets settled their few remaining differences in order to launch a joint attack on our own Galaxy—now positively identified as the source of the offending remark.

For thousands more years, the mighty ships tore across the empty wastes of space and finally dived screaming on to the first planet they came across—which happened to be the Earth—where due to a terrible miscalculation of scale the entire battle fleet was accidentally swallowed by a small dog.

Those who study the complex interplay of cause and effect in the history of the Universe say that this sort of thing is going on all the time, but that we are powerless to prevent it.

"It's just life," they say.

A short aircar trip brought Arthur and the old Magrathean to a doorway. They left the car and went through the door into a waiting room full of glass-topped tables and Plexiglas awards. Almost immediately, a light flashed above the door at the other side of the room and they entered.

"Arthur! You're safe!" a voice cried.

"Am I?" said Arthur, rather startled. "Oh, good."

The lighting was rather subdued and it took him a moment or so to see Ford, Trillian and Zaphod sitting round a large table beautifully decked out with exotic dishes, strange sweetmeats and bizarre fruits. They were stuffing their faces.

"What happened to you?" demanded Arthur.

"Well," said Zaphod, attacking a boneful of grilled muscle, "our guests here have been gassing us and zapping our minds and being generally weird and have now given us a rather nice meal to make it up to us. Here," he said, hoicking out a lump of evil-smelling meat from a bowl, "have some Vegan Rhino's cutlet. It's delicious if you happen to like that sort of thing."

"Hosts?" said Arthur. "What hosts? I don't see any . . ."

A small voice said, "Welcome to lunch, Earth creature."

Arthur glanced around and suddenly yelped.

"Ugh!" he said. "There are mice on the table!"

There was an awkward silence as everyone looked pointedly at Arthur.

He was busy staring at two white mice sitting in what looked like whisky glasses on the table. He heard the silence and glanced around at everyone.

"Oh!" he said, with sudden realization. "Oh, I'm sorry, I wasn't quite prepared for . . ."

"Let me introduce you," said Trillian. "Arthur, this is Benjy mouse."

"Hi," said one of the mice. His whiskers stroked what must have been a touch sensitive panel on the inside of the whisky glasslike affair, and it moved forward slightly.

"And this is Frankie mouse."

The other mouse said, "Pleased to meet you," and did likewise.

Arthur gaped.

"But aren't they . . ."

"Yes," said Trillian, "they are the mice I brought with me from the Earth."

She looked him in the eye and Arthur thought he detected the tiniest resigned shrug.

"Could you pass me that bowl of grated Arcturan Mega-Donkey?" she said.

Slartibartfast coughed politely.

"Er, excuse me," he said.

"Yes, thank you, Slartibartfast," said Benjy mouse sharply, "you may go."

"What? Oh . . . er, very well," said the old man, slightly taken aback, "I'll just go and get on with some of my fjords then."

"Ah, well, in fact that won't be necessary," said Frankie mouse. "It looks very much as if we won't be needing the new Earth any longer." He swiveled his pink little eyes. "Not now that we have found a native of the planet who was there seconds before it was destroyed."

"What?" cried Slartibartfast, aghast. "You can't mean that! I've got a thousand glaciers poised and ready to roll over Africa!"

"Well, perhaps you can take a quick skiing holiday before you dismantle them," said Frankie acidly.

"Skiing holiday!" cried the old man. "Those glaciers are works of art! Elegantly sculpted contours, soaring pinnacles of ice, deep majestic ravines! It would be sacrilege to go skiing on high art!"

"Thank you, Slartibartfast," said Benjy firmly. "That will be all."

"Yes, sir," said the old man coldly, "thank you very much. Well, goodbye, Earthman," he said to Arthur, "hope the life-style comes together."

With a brief nod to the rest of the company he turned and walked sadly out of the room.

Arthur stared after him, not knowing what to say.

"Now," said Benjy mouse, "to business."

Ford and Zaphod clinked their glasses together.

"To business!" they said.

"I beg your pardon?" said Benjy.

Ford looked round.

"Sorry, I thought you were proposing a toast," he said.

The two mice scuttled impatiently around in their glass transports. Finally they composed themselves, and Benjy moved forward to address Arthur.

"Now, Earth creature," he said, "the situation we have in effect is this. We have, as you know, been more or less running your planet for the last ten million years in order to find this wretched thing called the Ultimate Question."

"Why?" said Arthur sharply.

"No—we already thought of that one," said Frankie interrupting, "but it doesn't fit the answer. *Why? Forty-two* . . . you see, it doesn't work."

"No," said Arthur, "I mean, why have you been doing it?"

"Oh, I see," said Frankie. "Well, eventually just habit I think, to be brutally honest. And this is more or less the point—we're sick to the teeth with the whole thing, and the prospect of doing it all over again on account of those whinnet-ridden Vogons quite frankly gives me the screaming heebie-jeebies, you know what I mean? It was by the merest lucky chance that Benjy and I finished our particular job and left the planet early for a quick holiday, and have since manipulated our way back to Magrathea by the good offices of your friends."

"Magrathea is a gateway back to our own dimension," put in Benjy.

"Since when," continued his murine colleague, "we have had an offer of a quite enormously fat contract to do the 5D chat show and lecture circuit back in our own dimensional neck of the woods, and we're very much inclined to take it."

"I would, wouldn't you, Ford?" said Zaphod promptingly.

"Oh yes," said Ford, "jump at it, like a shot."

Arthur glanced at them, wondering what all this was leading up to.

"But we've got to have *product*, you see," said Frankie. "I mean, ideally we still need the Ultimate Question in some form or other."

Zaphod leaned forward to Arthur.

"You see," he said, "if they're just sitting there in the studio looking very relaxed and, you know, just mentioning that they happen to know the Answer to Life, the Universe and Everything, and then eventually have to admit that in fact it's Forty-two, then the show's probably quite short. No follow-up, you see."

"We have to have something that *sounds* good," said Benjy.

"Something that *sounds* good?" exclaimed Arthur. "An

Ultimate Question that *sounds* good? From a couple of mice?"

The mice bristled.

"Well, I mean, *yes* idealism, *yes* the dignity of pure research, *yes* the pursuit of truth in all its forms, but there comes a point I'm afraid where you begin to suspect that if there's any *real* truth, it's that the entire multidimensional infinity of the Universe is almost certainly being run by a bunch of maniacs. And if it comes to a choice between spending yet another ten million years finding that out, and on the other hand just taking the money and running, then I for one could do with the exercise," said Frankie.

"But . . ." started Arthur, hopelessly.

"Hey, will you get this, Earthman," interrupted Zaphod. "You are a last generation product of that computer matrix, right, and you were there right up to the moment your planet got the finger, yeah?"

"Er . . "

"So your brain was an organic part of the penultimate configuration of the computer program," said Ford, rather lucidly he thought.

"Right?" said Zaphod.

"Well," said Arthur doubtfully. He wasn't aware of ever having felt an organic part of anything. He had always seen this as one of his problems.

"In other words," said Benjy, steering his curious little vehicle right over to Arthur, "there's a good chance that the structure of the question is encoded in the structure of your brain—so we want to buy it off you."

"What, the question?" said Arthur.

"Yes," said Ford and Trillian.

"For lots of money," said Zaphod.

"No, no," said Frankie, "it's the brain we want to buy."

"What!"

"Well, who would miss it?" inquired Benjy.

"I thought you said you could just read his brain electronically," protested Ford.

"Oh yes," said Frankie, "but we'd have to get it out first. It's got to be prepared."

"Treated," said Benjy.

"Diced."

"Thank you," shouted Arthur, tipping up his chair and backing away from the table in horror.

"It could always be replaced," said Benjy reasonably, "if you think it's important."

"Yes, an electronic brain," said Frankie, "a simple one would suffice."

"A simple one!" wailed Arthur.

"Yeah," said Zaphod with a sudden evil grin, "you'd just have to program it to say *What?* and *I don't understand* and *Where's the tea?* Who'd know the difference?"

"What?" cried Arthur, backing away still farther.

"See what I mean?" said Zaphod, and howled with pain because of something that Trillian did at that moment.

"*I'd* notice the difference," said Arthur.

"No, you wouldn't," said Frankie mouse, "you'd be programmed not to."

Ford made for the door.

"Look, I'm sorry, mice, old lads," he said. "I don't think we've got a deal."

"I rather think we have to have a deal," said the mice in chorus, all the charm vanishing from their piping little voices in an instant. With a tiny whining shriek their two glass transports lifted themselves off the table, and swung through the air toward Arthur, who stumbled farther backward into a blind corner, utterly unable to cope or think of anything.

Trillian grabbed him desperately by the arm and tried to drag him toward the door, which Ford and Zaphod were struggling to open, but Arthur was deadweight—he seemed hypnotized by the airborne rodents swooping toward him.

She screamed at him, but he just gaped.

With one more yank, Ford and Zaphod got the door open. On the other side of it was a small pack of rather ugly men who they could only assume were the heavy mob of Magrathea. Not only were they ugly themselves, but the medical equipment they carried with them was also far from pretty. They charged.

So—Arthur was about to have his head cut open, Trillian was unable to help him and Ford and Zaphod were about to be set upon by several thugs a great deal heavier and more sharply armed than they were.

All in all it was extremely fortunate that at that moment every alarm on the planet burst into an ear-splitting din.

Chapter 32

Emergency! Emergency!" blared the klaxons throughout Magrathea. *"Hostile ship has landed on planet. Armed intruders in section 8A. Defense stations, defense stations!"*

The two mice sniffed irritably round the fragments of their glass transports where they lay shattered on the floor. "Damnation," muttered Frankie mouse, "all that fuss over two pounds of Earthling brain." He scuttled round and about, his pink eyes flashing, his fine white coat bristling with static. "The only thing we can do now," said Benjy, crouching and stroking his whiskers in thought, "is to try and fake a question, invent one that will sound plausible."

"Difficult," said Frankie. He thought. "How about *What's yellow and dangerous?*"

Benjy considered this for a moment.

"No, no good," he said. "Doesn't fit the answer."

They sank into silence for a few seconds.

"All right," said Benjy. *"What do you get if you multiply six by seven?"*

"No, no, too literal, too factual," said Frankie, "wouldn't sustain the punters' interest."

Again they thought.

Then Frankie said, "Here's a thought. *How many roads must a man walk down?*"

"Ah!" said Benjy. "Aha, now that does sound promising!" He rolled the phrase around a little. "Yes," he said, "that's excellent! Sounds very significant without actually tying you down to meaning anything at all. *How many roads must a man walk down? Forty-two.* Excellent, excellent, that'll fox 'em. Frankie, baby, we are made!"

They performed a scampering dance in their excitement.

Near them on the floor lay several rather ugly men who had been hit about the head with some heavy design awards.

Half a mile away, four figures pounded up a corridor looking for a way out. They emerged into a wide open-plan computer bay. They glanced about wildly.

"Which way you reckon, Zaphod?" said Ford.

"At a wild guess, I'd say down here," said Zaphod, running off down to the right between a computer bank and the wall. As the others started after him he was brought up short by a Kill-O-Zap energy bolt that cracked through the air inches in front of him and fried a small section of adjacent wall.

A voice on a bullhorn said, "Okay, Beeblebrox, hold it right there. We've got you covered."

"Cops!" hissed Zaphod, and spun around in a crouch. "You want to try a guess at all, Ford?"

"Okay, this way," said Ford, and the four of them ran down a gangway between two computer banks.

At the end of the gangway appeared a heavily armored

and space-suited figure waving a vicious Kill-O-Zap gun.

"We don't want to shoot you, Beeblebrox!" shouted the figure.

"Suits me fine!" shouted Zaphod back, and dived down a wide gap between two data process units.

The others swerved in behind him.

"There are two of them," said Trillian. "We're cornered."

They squeezed themselves down in an angle between a large computer data bank and the wall.

They held their breath and waited.

Suddenly the air exploded with energy bolts as both the cops opened fire on them simultaneously.

"Hey, they're shooting at us," said Arthur, crouching in a tight ball. "I thought they said they didn't want to do that."

"Yeah, *I* thought they said that," agreed Ford.

Zaphod stuck a head up for a dangerous moment.

"Hey," he said, "I thought you said you didn't want to shoot us!" and ducked again.

They waited.

After a moment a voice replied, "It isn't easy being a cop!"

"What did he say?" whispered Ford in astonishment.

"He said it isn't easy being a cop."

"Well, surely that's his problem, isn't it?"

"I'd have thought so."

Ford shouted out, "Hey, listen! I think we've got enough problems of our own having you shooting at us, so if you could avoid laying *your* problems on us as well, I think we'd all find it easier to cope!"

Another pause, and then the bullhorn again.

"Now see here, guy," said the voice, "you're not dealing with any dumb two-bit trigger-pumping morons with low hairlines, little piggy eyes and no conversation, we're a couple of intelligent caring guys that you'd probably quite like if you met us socially! I don't go around gratuitously shooting people and then bragging about it afterward in seedy space-rangers bars, like some cops I could mention! I go around shooting people gratuitously and then I agonize about it afterward for hours to my girlfriend!"

"And I write novels!" chimed in the other cop. "Though I haven't had any of them published yet, so I better warn you, I'm in a *meeeean* mood!"

Ford's eyes popped halfway out of their sockets. "Who are these guys?" he said.

"Dunno," said Zaphod, "I think I preferred it when they were shooting."

"So are you going to come quietly," shouted one of the cops again, "or are you going to let us blast you out?"

"Which would you prefer?" shouted Ford.

A millisecond later the air about them started to fry again, as bolt after bolt of Kill-O-Zap hurled itself into the computer bank in front of them.

The fusillade continued for several seconds at unbearable intensity.

When it stopped, there were a few seconds of near-quietness as the echoes died away.

"You still there?" called one of the cops.

"Yes," they called back.

"We didn't enjoy doing that at all," shouted the other cop.

"We could tell," shouted Ford.

"Now, listen to this, Beeblebrox, and you better listen good!"

"Why?" shouted back Zaphod.

"Because," shouted the cop, "it's going to be very intelligent, and quite interesting and humane! Now—either you all give yourselves up now and let us beat you up a bit, though not very much of course because we are firmly opposed to needless violence, or we blow up this entire planet and possibly one or two others we noticed on our way out here!"

"But that's crazy!" cried Trillian. "You wouldn't do that!"

"Oh yes, we would," shouted the cop, "wouldn't we?" he asked the other one.

"Oh yes, we'd have to, no question," the other one called back.

"But why?" demanded Trillian.

"Because there are some things you have to do even if you are an enlightened liberal cop who knows all about sensitivity and everything!"

"I just don't believe these guys," muttered Ford, shaking his head.

One cop shouted to the other, "Shall we shoot them again for a bit?"

"Yeah, why not?"

They let fly another electric barrage.

The heat and noise was quite fantastic. Slowly, the computer bank was beginning to disintegrate. The front had almost all melted away, and thick rivulets of molten metal were winding their way back toward where they were squatting. They huddled farther back and waited for the end.

Chapter 33

But the end never came, at least not then.

Quite suddenly the barrage stopped, and the sudden silence afterward was punctuated by a couple of strangled gurgles and thuds.

The four stared at each other.

"What happened?" said Arthur.

"They stopped," said Zaphod with a shrug.

"Why?"

"Dunno, do you want to go and ask them?"

"No."

They waited.

"Hello?" called out Ford.

No answer.

"That's odd."

"Perhaps it's a trap."

"They haven't the wit."

"What were those thuds?"

"Dunno."

They waited for a few more seconds.

"Right," said Ford, "I'm going to have a look."

He glanced round at the others.

"Is no one going to say, *No, you can't possibly, let me go instead?*"

They all shook their heads.

"Oh well," he said, and stood up.

For a moment, nothing happened.

Then, after a second or so, nothing continued to happen. Ford peered through the thick smoke that was billowing out of the burning computer.

Cautiously he stepped out into the open.

Still nothing happened.

Twenty yards away he could dimly see through the smoke the space-suited figure of one of the cops. He was lying in a crumpled heap on the ground. Twenty yards in the other direction lay the second man. No one else was anywhere to be seen.

This struck Ford as being extremely odd.

Slowly, nervously, he walked toward the first one. The body lay reassuringly still as he approached it, and continued to lie reassuringly still as he reached it and put his foot down on the Kill-O-Zap gun that still dangled from its limp fingers.

He reached down and picked it up, meeting no resistance.

The cop was quite clearly dead.

A quick examination revealed him to be from Blagulon Kappa—he was a methane-breathing life form, dependent on his space suit for survival in the thin oxygen atmosphere of Magrathea.

The tiny life-support system computer on his backpack appeared unexpectedly to have blown up.

Ford poked around in it in considerable astonishment. These miniature suit computers usually had the full back-up of the main computer back on the ship, with which they were directly linked through the sub-etha. Such a system was fail-safe in all circumstances other than total feedback malfunction, which was unheard of.

He hurried over to the other prone figure, and discovered that exactly the same impossible thing had happened to him, presumably simultaneously.

He called the others over to look. They came, shared his astonishment, but not his curiosity.

"Let's get shot of this hole," said Zaphod. "If whatever I'm supposed to be looking for is here, I don't want it." He grabbed the second Kill-O-Zap gun, blasted a perfectly harmless accounting computer and rushed out into the corridor, followed by the others. He very nearly blasted hell out of an aircar that stood waiting for them a few yards away. The aircar was empty, but Arthur recognized it as belonging to Slartibartfast.

It had a note from him pinned to part of its sparse instrument panel. The note had an arrow drawn on it, pointing at one of the controls.

It said, *This is probably the best button to press.*

Chapter 34

The aircar rocketed them at speeds in excess of R17 through the steel tunnels that led out on to the appalling surface of the planet which was now in the grip of yet another drear morning twilight. Ghastly gray light congealed on the land.

R is a velocity measure, defined as a reasonable speed of travel that is consistent with health, mental well-being and not being more than, say, five minutes late. It is therefore clearly an almost infinitely variable figure according to circumstances, since the first two factors vary not only with speed taken as an absolute, but also with awareness of the third factor. Unless handled with tranquillity this equation can result in considerable stress, ulcers and even death.

R17 is not a fixed velocity, but it is clearly far too fast.

The aircar flung itself through the air at R17 and above, deposited them next to the Heart of Gold which stood starkly on the frozen ground like a bleached bone, and then precipitately hurled itself back in the direction whence they had come, presumably on important business of its own.

Shivering, the four of them stood and looked at the ship.

Beside it stood another one.

It was the Blagulon Kappa policecraft, a bulbous shark-like affair, slate-green in color and smothered with black stenciled letters of varying degrees of size and unfriendliness. The letters informed anyone who cared to read them as to where the ship was from, what section of the police it was assigned to, and where the power feeds should be connected.

It seemed somehow unnaturally dark and silent, even for a ship whose two-man crew was at that moment lying asphyxiated in a smoke-filled chamber several miles beneath the ground. It is one of those curious things that is impossible to explain or define, but one can sense when a ship is completely dead.

Ford could sense it and found it most mysterious—a ship and two policemen seemed to have gone spontaneously dead. In his experience the Universe simply didn't work like that.

The other three could sense it too, but they could sense the bitter cold even more and hurried back into the Heart of Gold suffering from an acute attack of no curiosity.

Ford stayed, and went to examine the Blagulon ship. As he walked, he nearly tripped over an inert steel figure lying face down in the cold dust.

"Marvin!" he exclaimed. "What are you doing?"

"Don't feel you have to take any notice of me, please," came a muffled drone.

"But how are you, metalman?" said Ford.

"Very depressed."

"What's up?"

"I don't know," said Marvin, "I've never been there."

"Why," said Ford squatting down beside him and shivering. "are you lying face down in the dust?"

"It's a very effective way of being wretched," said Marvin. "Don't pretend you want to talk to me, I know you hate me."

"No, I don't."

"Yes, you do, everybody does. It's part of the shape of the Universe. I only have to talk to somebody and they begin to hate me. Even robots hate me. If you just ignore me I expect I shall probably go away."

He jacked himself up to his feet and stood resolutely facing the opposite direction.

"That ship hated me," he said dejectedly, indicating the policecraft.

"That ship?" said Ford in sudden excitement. "What happened to it? Do you know?"

"It hated me because I talked to it."

"You *talked* to it?" exclaimed Ford. "What do you mean you talked to it?"

"Simple. I got very bored and depressed, so I went and plugged myself in to its external computer feed. I talked to the computer at great length and explained my view of the Universe to it," said Marvin.

"And what happened?" pressed Ford.

"It committed suicide," said Marvin, and stalked off back to the Heart of Gold.

Chapter 35

That night, as the Heart of Gold was busy putting a few light-years between itself and the Horsehead Nebula, Zaphod lounged under the small palm tree on the bridge trying to bang his brain into shape with massive Pan Galactic Gargle Blasters; Ford and Trillian sat in a corner discussing life and matters arising from it; and Arthur took to his bed to flip through Ford's copy of *The Hitchhiker's Guide to the Galaxy*. Since he was going to have to live in the place, he reasoned, he'd better start finding out something about it.

He came across this entry.

It said: *"The History of every major Galactic Civilization tends to pass through three distinct and recognizable phases, those of Survival, Inquiry and Sophistication, otherwise known as the How, Why and Where phases.*

"For instance, the first phase is characterized by the question How can we eat? *the second by the question* Why do we eat? *and the third by the question* Where shall we have lunch?"

He got no further before the ship's intercom buzzed into life.

"Hey, Earthman? You hungry, kid?" said Zaphod's voice.

"Er, well, yes, a little peckish, I suppose," said Arthur.

"Okay, baby, hold tight," said Zaphod. "We'll take in a quick bite at the Restaurant at the End of the Universe."

And It Came to Pass, to Arthur Dent on the Worst Thursday That Ever Happened . . .

England no longer existed. He'd got that—somehow he'd got it. He tried again. America, he thought, has gone. He couldn't grasp it. He decided to start smaller again. New York has gone. No reaction. He'd never seriously believed it existed anyway. The dollar, he thought, has sunk for ever. Slight tremor there. Every Bogart movie has been wiped, he said to himself, and that gave him a nasty knock. McDonald's, he thought. There is no longer any such thing as a McDonald's hamburger.

He passed out. When he came round a second later he found he was sobbing for his mother.

"Extremely funny . . . inspired lunacy . . . over much too soon. But don't panic—there's a sequel on the way!"
—*Washington Post Book World*